JOHNIE

IRISH

When doing the right thing isn't the right thing to do...

T.N. Jones

PHOENIX JONES PUBLISHING LLC

JOHNIE IRISH

Copyright © 2021 by Tomara Jones.

This book is a work of fiction. Names, characters, businesses, organiza- tions, places, events and incidents either are the product of the author's imagination or are used fictitiously. Any resemblance to actual persons, living or dead, events, or locales is entirely coincidental.

For information contact :

Info@phoenixjonespublishing.com

http://www.phoenixjonespublishing.com

Book Formatting by Derek Murphy @Creativindie

Book and Cover design by Phoenix Jones Publishing, LLC

Photography by Alex Azabache

ISBN: 978-0-9911055-6-4

10 9 8 7 6 5 4 3 2 1

1

BAYER THOMPSON STOOD ON A random street in Brooklyn, New York, with his son Cory by his side. Red, yellow, and brown leaves scattered across the sidewalk at their feet. Bayer's height and muscular frame made him wider than most, a formidable and intimidating man to nearly everyone he encountered. He tried his best to shield that energy from his son. On the other hand, Cory mimicked his father's handsome features while the rest of his character was far more approachable, especially at half the size of his dad.

Cory's car idled on the curb while they took in the October morning's crisp autumn breeze. The warmth of the hot coffee cup in Bayer's hand soothed him as he watched cars drive up and impossible. Who would fund him? Who would work with him?

The thoughts flooding his mind would be enough to drive anyone mad, but Bayer took several deep breaths running his hands over the waves spiraling his head.

"One step at a time," he mumbled to himself. So Bayer did just that. He took one step at a time where his son's words continued to echo through the labyrinth of his mind. All he could do was a laugh to himself, "Story of my life."

2

The office of Genevieve Parsons smelled like the softest hints of lavender as Bayer stepped inside. Shelves of books took up the entire wall behind her while her degrees, certifications, and pictures of her with high-ranking politicians and officials decorated the wall to the right of her desk.

By the time she reached her 35th birthday, she'd been offered several promotions but refused them as her calling was to remain a parole officer. It had its drawbacks, but when people like Bayer Thompson landed in her office, she found her position worthwhile. Right now, however, after the story he'd just told her, she was infuriated.

"What was that plate number again?" she asked, searching her scattered desk for a pen. She jotted down the numerals Bayer spouted before plopping into her chair and shuffling the mouse around on her desk. She typed a few keystrokes before turning to him with worry in her eyes, "And you said you heard him say, 'Holcomb'?"

"Yeah," Bayer sighed, "The radio blasted a call through. He picked it up, said Holcomb, and then cursed me out before peeling down the street with my ID in his visor."

"Shit!" Genevieve cursed under her breath as she clicked through screens, "Detective Leon Holcomb of the one nine has a serious hardon for Sinclair and Irish. And you're still standing by your non-affiliation to Sinclair, right?"

Bayer rolled his eyes, "Don't do this to me, please. Right now, you're one of the few people not related to me who I trust and who trust me. I need to get that ID back. I have an interview tomorrow and won't get access to the Wilhelm Offices without the picture ID. I'm fucking screwed!

I need that job!"

"Maybe not," she sighed, "I can vouch for you."

Bayer held his hand up, "You've done more than enough for me, Gen. Honestly, though, my PO vouching for me at a tech conglomerate doesn't scream hire me."

"I don't recommend going to retrieve it. You might have to look for something else. I'll give you another extension to find employment."

"NO!" Bayer slammed his hands against the desk, startling her. He closed his eyes, rubbing the bridge of his nose, letting out a deep exhale before sitting back in his seat.

The worried gaze of Genevieve Parsons mirrored Bayer's distress. She shattered expectations of what he expected a parole officer to be. He'd heard horror stories, but she was like an angel sent to help him. Her beauty exuded from the inside out with her dark brown coily hair always pinned in a simple, elegant design. It eased his anxiety to have a successful black woman as his parole officer. There were things he didn't have to explain. There were things she just understood. But, at this moment, she wasn't understanding.

"He doesn't get to get away with this, Gen. I don't want you doing extra anything because this officer doesn't have his facts straight. I'm not working for Sinclair. The last time I even spoke to him was on a visit five years ago. He thanked me, and that was it. I told you this. I told everyone this. This shit is just frustrating when all I wanna do is live my fucking life. I want to mind my business and move on."

"I know that, Bayer, but I think you need to let this go. Holcomb doesn't even need a reason to put you in cuffs. I don't want to put you through the system, but if you don't give me a choice, I have to do my job. Please don't make me violate you.

Leave Detective Leon Holcomb alone! Hell, go get a fake ID until a real one comes from the DMV."

"You're advising me to break the law," Bayer smirked.

"Bend it. It's a temporary fix. It's not like you'll be using completely false information. I'll send you my scanned copy of it, and you take it to someone and…"

Bayer leaned forward with a genuine smile on his face, "I don't know anyone who does that stuff."

He did have a few people he could call. If he called in a few favors, he could probably get in front of a computer and make one himself, but that's information he didn't need to share with his parole officer. Not to mention, those were favors he wasn't ready to cash in.

Bayer continued to smile as he told her, "I don't have any ties to the criminal world. I was on the straight and narrow before I went in. I was on the straight and narrow, for the most part, while I did my time. And I'm desperately trying to do that now. Doing the right thing has done nothing but fuck me. I got my girlfriend pregnant when I was 15, got a job, finished school, married her, and what? She cheats on me, divorces me, gets alimony, child support, and refuses to remarry so she can continue to collect alimony even though she's been with this guy for over a decade. I start my own business, grow it successfully, go out to celebrate with colleagues, and guess what?"

"I know the story, Bayer."

"No, just listen, listen. I come out of the club, ask a few guys a question about a hotel, and take my black ass to my car when I see this girl getting knocked around. I do the right thing and defend this lady, but that shit gets all twisted up by the DA, and I go in for two counts of manslaughter. The girl disappeared, and I'm lucky they didn't pin that on me too. Now, I'm out.

I'm doing everything that's being asked of me, and with four months down, I get stopped by some dick who wants to flash his badge over some shit I have nothing to do with?

He said I was one of Sinclair's favorite goons, but that doesn't make any sense. You know it doesn't! I've been in a room twice with Cesar Sinclair, and only once have I ever looked him in his eyes. I do not know him or the other guy Irish! But fuck me for doing the right thing and keeping my mouth shut. Fuck me for helping that girl and taking responsibility for what I did. I'm fucked! Look me in the eyes, Genevieve, and tell me I'm not!"

The parole officer propped up her forehead on her fingertips with her elbows anchored to the desk. She couldn't look her parolee in the eyes because he was right. Doing the right thing has done nothing but bite him in the ass, but she didn't want to see him do something to get himself locked up or force him to finish out the remainder of his sentence behind bars.

Refusing to match his gaze, she spoke firmly, "Please, do not poke the bear. Leave Detective Holcomb alone. I'm advising you to get a temporary ID from wherever you can to secure employment tomorrow. Do not provoke that guy into putting cuffs on you. You will violate your parole if that happens."

"Fine, I won't provoke him, but I want this all on the record that I came here directly after interacting with an officer. I complied with his orders and yours. I'm going to the DMV now to see what I can do by tomorrow."

"Thank you," Genevieve let out a sigh of relief. "I'll extend your curfew tonight since you're going to the DMV, and that's gonna take a while. I expect to hear your voice tonight from your home, not from the one-nine holding tank. You got me?"

"I got you," Bayer nodded.

He liked Genevieve from the moment they met. Her beauty astounded him, and after the work she'd put in to make sure he didn't violate his parole, their relationship was one of the few good things he could hold onto. So he decided to try and do the right thing one more time.

3

The 19th precinct sat in the middle of a one-way street in Bay Ridge; in that part of Brooklyn way too close to Staten Island, New York. Even though Bayer could see the Verrazano Bridge from where he stood, he still felt a long way from home. He stood outside with his hands in his pockets, watching cops walk in and out of the heavy wooden doors up a short flight of steps. A nagging feeling kept tugging at the nape of his neck like an itch he couldn't scratch. He pushed himself forward.

Once inside, Bayer approached the desk sergeant cautiously. The man who sat in front of him had a pleasant demeanor, smiling at Bayer. "Good afternoon. How can I help you?"

"Um," Bayer hesitated. He didn't want to be

inside of this precinct, or any precinct for that matter. Fuck doing the right thing. Taking a deep breath, he shook his head, "Never mind, just forget I was here."

He turned around to leave when he was greeted by the grinning face of Detective Holcomb, "Well, look what the fucking cat dragged in. Are you following me?"

Bayer spoke softly, making sure to keep his hands in the officer's field of vision, "I came here to get my ID back, but just forget it."

"No," Holcomb delightfully responded, "You came all the way down here. Let's get it back to you. Follow me."

Dread washed over Bayer as he wanted to turn and run, but that would stir up a commotion he didn't want to incite. He followed Holcomb through a glass door to the right of the reception area. A long hallway that held doors on both sides made

Bayer's gut twist in anxiety. He should have listened to Genevieve.

Holcomb walked into a large office that held three desks. A large whiteboard contained pictures, pages, and other kinds of information pinned to it. There were shelves of books, boxes of folders, and file cabinets, all of which gave the appearance of a disorganized system. There was only one other person in the room, Detective Israel Jessup, who looked up at Holcomb and Bayer with perplexity in his eyes before returning his attention to the pages on his desk.

"I shouldn't be here," Bayer mumbled, "I'm sorry for intruding, Sir. Just forget it."

"No, no, no!" Holcomb exaggerated, "Let me roll out the red carpet for you! I can't believe Irish had the audacity to send you down here."

"No one sent me down here," Bayer sighed, rubbing the bridge of his nose, "You took my ID, and I need it back. I have an interview tomorrow and-"

Holcomb didn't let him finish, "What? The Sinclair Syndicate requires their men to carry identifying pieces of government-issued information? That doesn't make much sense, Thompson."

The mention of Bayer's name piqued Israel's interest, who'd been sitting at the desk quietly. The two men who recently disturbed his silence now had his full attention.

"None of this makes sense," Bayer relented, "I just want my ID so I can get a job and move out of my kid's house. Please, Detective."

"Why don't you ask your boss for a raise? Or perhaps one of his shell companies has some real estate you can move into," Holcomb's incessant prodding nearly made Bayer lose his cool.

"For the last time, I don't work for Cesar

Sinclair or anyone named Irish. I don't even know these guys! I did my time, and I'm just trying to do the right thing!"

Holcomb raised an eyebrow, "You see, that's what doesn't make sense to me. You just said you did your time, but you didn't. How does someone like you, who's not in with the Sinclair Syndicate, get a temporary release to attend a wedding? How does someone who's supposed to serve a 16-year sentence for two counts of manslaughter get out in six? That seems lucky for someone without a boss with some deep pockets to push your processing through the system a shit lot quicker than other criminals who've committed lesser crimes. And you're not here now to get information about the case I'm working on?"

"Man, you took my ID while I was on my way to parole this morning. You're the only reason I'm here! Please just give me my ID back."

Bayer was a step above begging to make this

trip worth it. Holcomb pulled Bayer's ID out of his pocket.

"Motherfucker," Bayer growled under his breath.

"This is what you're here for, huh?" Holcomb waved the ID in front of Bayer's face. Bayer knew better than to take the bait. Detective Leon Holcomb waved the ID around like he was about to do a magic trick. He practically danced over to a large bin with a thin slot running across its lid, dropped the ID in it, and hit a red switch. The excruciating noise of Bayer's ID being decimated by the industrial paper shredder made a vein pulse just above his eyebrow.

"Ta-da," Holcomb sang with restrained laughter. "Abracadabra motherfucker. Get the fuck out of my precinct. I don't have your fucking ID."

Bayer wanted to wrap his fingers around Holcomb's throat and squeeze the life out of him.

But, Bayer did what he did best; he hushed his inner beast and left the precinct.

Detective Holcomb leaned against his desk with his arms folded across his chest. Israel finally spoke, "You're a real asshole, Leon."

"Fuck him, Sinclair, and Irish. I'm going to break that guy. He's gonna flip on Sinclair. Watch." Holcomb's certainty radiated from his narrowed gaze.

Israel pushed himself away from his desk and walked over to the file cabinet. He dug around the drawer for a moment before pulling the thinnest folder out of the bunch. He waved it in front of Holcomb's face.

"You know how many pages are in this file?" Israel asked the brooding Detective Holcomb.

"Never bothered to count," Holcomb shrugged.

"There are ten pages in here, max. Bayer

Thompson was railroaded. He did his time. I've seen the footage from the club that night, just like you. This guy's never had so much as a parking ticket. He has no history, just the wrong place, wrong time, and should've called the cops instead of taking matters into his own hands. He ain't take one look at that board with Sinclair's mugshot plastered all over it. He didn't try to take a picture covertly. He didn't touch anything in here. He spoke to you and only you. I believe him when he says he doesn't work for Sinclair or Irish. He's not on any agency's list of known associates. You gotta let this go. He's not a player."

Detective Holcomb ran his tongue over his teeth, sucking in air through them like he was trying to remove something stuck under his gums. His arms bulged, flexing in frustration, "I don't care what that asshole says! He's a player, whether he realizes it or not, and he's fucking up. He's got a shit ton more to lose than anyone in Sinclair's organization."

"That's my point," Israel shook his head, "Everyone we've ever fingered working for them has no family. No wives. No kids. No girlfriends. They're expendable and ruthless because there's very little that can be taken from them and because they want to be. Irish, especially, has a knack for hiring sociopaths, and this guy Bayer doesn't fit in. What are you gonna do, Leon?"

Detective Holcomb fumed, "Bayer's going to bring me, Sinclair. Even if he doesn't know that yet."

4

Bayer made his way to the DMV, filed his paperwork, and left with a paper receipt. The day didn't end as planned, and by the time he made it to a quiet street on a forgetful block in Staten Island, his feet ached. With his energy depleted, he stood in front of a ranch house with a small structure in the back. It used to be a garage before Cory converted it into a studio apartment for him.

Bayer walked by the SUV parked in front of a small sedan. He smiled, seeing it backed in. Every night Cory would back his wife's truck out of the driveway to turn it around so she could drive straight out every morning. He made sure to fill her gas tank and kept the maintenance up-to-date. Cory kept his wife's new truck in perfect condition while driving his used sedan wherever he needed to go.

Bayer couldn't be any prouder of how his son matured into a man. The kitchen light was on. Shadows of the young couple enjoying dinner together warmed his heart. He elected to leave them be, making his way toward the apartment behind the house.

As soon as he stepped inside, the phone rang. He knew it was Genevieve. She never missed a check-in. He grabbed the phone off the hook, "Officer Parsons."

The audible sigh of relief made him grin, "I was really hoping you'd be there."

"I'm here, just walked in. I was about to sit down to dinner. How about you?"

"I'm going to head home soon. I have a few more things to wrap up at my office, and then I'll be able to enjoy a ready-made entree made from the best chefs at Chez de Burger King."

Bayer laughed, "That's no meal for a hard-working woman like yourself. How would you feel about-"

"Bayer, don't," she practically whispered. "We can't, and you know that."

"But if we could, would you?" he asked her.

She paused for what seemed like an eternity. "The most I'll say is that any woman who has your attention is a lucky one and would be crazy not to give you a shot."

"So what does that make you?"

"Crazy about my job. I'm going to finish up here. I'll see you in a week, Thompson."

"Good night, Genevieve." Bayer heard the slightest moan, ripe with sexual tension, come through the receiver before the line disconnected.

He smiled.

Bayer made himself comfortable tossing his boots off his feet and into the corner near the door. While a part of him wondered what his daughter-in-law made for dinner, he stuck to the leftovers in his fridge. He turned on the TV for light, letting a movie watch him as he drummed over the events of the day. It didn't take long before a soft knock at his door disrupted him.

When Bayer opened the door, he expected to see Cory there with a cigarette in hand. Instead, he found Claire standing with a warm dish in oven mitts. She forced a smile before tilting her head slightly, waiting for Bayer to welcome her. He closed his eyes, acknowledging the peace she'd brought to his son's life while stepping to the side for her to come in.

"I thought you'd be hungry, Bayer," she spoke in a soothing tone he felt he never deserved.

"Thank you, sweetie. I wanted to give you and Cory your time together. I just got in a little while ago."

"I figured you were home when I didn't get a call from Officer Parsons," Claire raised an eyebrow.

Bayer stared at her waiting for Claire to continue.

"May I sit?" Claire motioned to the small loveseat in front of Bayer's bed. The entire space opened up. It didn't need walls as he was the only person who lived inside of the converted garage.

Bayer waved his hand in front of the sofa, offering her a seat. Claire was intelligent, brilliant even. She sat poised and elegant with her hair cut short just above her ears. He could see all of the reasons why his son loved her. He, himself, would do anything to protect her and his son.

"That should take about ten minutes to warm

up," Claire nodded her head toward the dish in the oven. "Enough time for us to have a little chat."

Bayer sulked, his shoulders slumped, and he pulled a chair away from his dining set to sit across from her. "What's on your mind?"

"Cory thinks the world of you. I love you, too," Claire's voice didn't have an ounce of trepidation. "But, after the visit I got today, I have to say something. Cory told me not to worry about it that it isn't about anything, but-"

"What visit, Claire?"

"A Detective Holcomb came by as soon as I got in from my shift. My intuition tells me he knows what time I come home from work. He had a few interesting things to tell me."

Bayer ran his hands over his face, "I'm sorry, Claire. This guy, Holcomb, he's nuts."

"Yeah, I'd say so. He thinks you're working for

Cesar Sinclair. I know you're not because you'd never betray your son, your daughter, or their trust in you. We have to have trust for this to work. Isn't that what we agreed on when you moved in here?"

"That's exactly what we agreed upon," Bayer conceded. "I don't want either of you getting mixed up in anything, so I'm leaving Detective Holcomb alone. He thinks I work for Sinclair, but I don't."

"You cannot bring whatever's chasing you here," Claire warned him. "Cory." The pause in her voice, shaking at the mere mention of her love's name, "Cory is so jaded when it comes to you."

Bayer nodded with sadness in his eyes. "Believe me; I know that."

"He's so proud of you being the man who always does the right thing. I love your son with every fiber of my being, but we both know I'm the realist in this relationship. The world doesn't always reward those people who do the right thing. Cory still believes your conviction can be overturned."

"My boy's always been a dreamer. I imagine that's how he snagged you," Bayer grinned.

Claire blushed, smoothing a coiled piece of hair behind her ear, "Yeah, but Cory's dreams for his wife and future are far more realistic than the dreams he has for his father. He holds you on such a high pedestal like you can do no wrong, but he's failing to realize some things are out of your control. Bayer, I'm scared. If you saw that look in Detective Holcomb's eyes, something is off."

"I saw the look in his eyes when he hemmed me up against a wall this morning. He's got an itch to scratch with this Sinclair thing, but I promise you, I have nothing to do with any of that. I've done nothing illegal since I've been home, and I won't."

"Okay," Claire sighed, "I believe you. I love you,

Bayer. But, I need you to do something for us."

"I'm out of here as soon as I find a place."

"Thank you." Claire's relief for Bayer not making her say the words was palpable. "Cory doesn't know I'm asking this."

"I know," Bayer nodded, "He doesn't have the sense to see around the corner as you do. Holcomb is going to be a problem no matter what I do. He thinks I'm tied to Sinclair and some guy named Irish. I can't figure out how to change his mind."

"The easiest way to do that is to stay on the path you're on. Continue being the man Cory and I both know you are. I'm sure this will pass. And, when it does, you're more than welcome to live here again if you don't find something you like."

Bayer Thompson watched his daughter-in-law move into his kitchen to remove the warmed dish from the oven before letting herself out. The world doesn't always reward people for doing the right thing. He's been the poster boy for that truth. The realization that the world around him would never do the right thing by him was a hard pill to swallow, but it didn't stop him from wanting to do right by his son. So Bayer ate his dinner with one goal in mind, to do the right thing one more time.

5

Detective Leon Holcomb sat in a black SUV in the middle of a quiet street somewhere in Staten Island. The cold autumn morning made his navy blue wool beanie necessary. The black hoodie and leather jacket served two purposes as he slid down to blend into his seat, letting his tinted windows shield him from the outside world. He didn't bother to shut his engine off as he watched people come and go from a large house that sat behind an iron gate held in place by stone posts. The gate stood about four feet high and seemed to wrap around the entire block.

The longer Holcomb sat there, the more he realized this particular block was more like a community within a community. Five other homes with beautiful yards sat within those stone posts and wrought iron fences which explained the amount of traffic coming in and out of the property. He didn't want to be there long. His gaze shifted to the files he stole from his precinct, spread out in the passenger seat next to him, riddled with mugshots of Eastern European gangsters.

Patience became one of his most beloved qualities as he waited for one individual in particular to show their smug face. When they finally emerged from the house, laughing with two others, he ducked down as they walked to a car parked a few spaces in front of him. As soon as the car pulled into the street, Holcomb followed them.

The mobsters never signaled Holcomb their awareness of his tail as he drove over the bridge into an affluent area of Brooklyn and parked in front of a Hungarian restaurant. He watched the three men head inside and nearly jumped out of his skin when his phone rang, disrupting his surveillance.

"Holcomb here," he answered, practically whispering.

"Are you running late or something?" Detective Israel Jessup poised the question with a tone wanting to know why rather than a straightforward yes or no.

"Something like that," Holcomb grinned. "Matter of fact, tell the sergeant I'm taking the day."

"What are you doing?" Israel's frustration vibrated through the line.

"I'm getting Sinclair brought to us," Holcomb replied.

"Whatever it is you're doing, stop it. This isn't the way to do this, Leon. You're cutting every other agency off at the knees. We have the IRS, Secret Service, DEA, ATF, and the FBI all working cohesively to bring down the Sinclair Syndicate.

Whatever your plan is, it doesn't sound like you're bringing down the entire organization. It sounds like a personal vendetta against the head of a criminal enterprise. You will not win this fight by yourself! Whatever you're doing, cut that shit out and bring your ass in! We got work to do."

"I'll come in," Holcomb relented, "Just let me take care of this one errand. I'll even bring you breakfast."

"Whatever," Israel grumbled before hanging up.

Holcomb didn't care what his fellow detective thought as he pushed himself out of the driver's seat, making his way toward the restaurant. It was barely nine when the bell chimed above the eatery's door. A few tables sat empty with the chairs turned upside down onto them. There was a small bar with a few stools in front. Two men sat there with drinks in their hands before turning to address Holcomb.

One of them shouted, "Hey buddy, we're closed, man. Come back after 12."

Holcomb made sure to leave his badge in the car as he pulled his beanie down over his brows to help mask his face. He wasn't going to take long as he pulled his gun from its holster. The guys shouted as they sprung out of their seats with their hands in the air.

"Man, ain't no money in the register. We're not even open yet," one of them stated.

"I ain't here to rob you," Holcomb hissed, trying to disguise his voice with an exaggerated New York accent that he probably heard from an 80s movie. "I got a message for your boss, yo. Tell him it takes more than a manslaughter rap to keep me off his back! He can't have his goons beat on women and think he's gonna get away with it. I'm always gonna come for him."

Holcomb let off a shot in the small space

shattering the mirrored glass behind the bar to make his point. He left just as quickly as he came in, ran to the still running SUV, and drove off in time to see the men run out of the restaurant trying to locate him. The vehicle blended into the morning traffic perfectly.

Holcomb counted on his complexion being close enough to Bayer's that they'd think he was the criminal parolee. The only thing he had to do was wait for the heat to come down onto Bayer and for Bayer to go running to Sinclair for backup. The plan was perfect. Once Sinclair came out of hiding to help Bayer, Holcomb was sure he could nab the both of them and send them to prison.

*****

Bayer Thompson stood on a crowded city block somewhere in Midtown Manhattan. The skyscraper waiting for him to step inside dwarfed the buildings around it while he nervously thought of the DMV paper receipt he held in his wallet masquerading as his ID.

The Wilhelm Offices held one of the largest tech marketing firms in the city. He'd be taking a massive pay cut from his role as CEO of a consulting firm. At this moment, Bayer only wanted that tick mark next to his name, identifying him as an employee. Starting over meant having to start from somewhere.

Bayer's suit didn't fit as well as it used to and a quick dry-cleaning got rid of the smell clinging to it from the storage unit he'd dug it out of. His pulse quickened with sweaty palms as he stood outside of the building willing his anxiety to settle down. This wasn't like him. The confident Mr. Thompson who built and ran TomTech Consultants no longer existed. Well, he did; he just had an enormous amount of stress standing on top of the cockiness he used to own.

Bayer kept his promise to himself to attempt to do the right thing. A deep inhale brought him scents of smoke, cars, and salted peanuts wafting in the city air. He wanted Claire to feel safe in her home, and he knew Cory wanted his wife happy. The easiest thing for him to do was get a decent-paying job and find another place to live. A place so Detective Holcomb wouldn't just pop up at his son's house.

The lobby of the Wilhelm Offices seemed too grey for Bayer's liking. He adjusted his attitude, strolling up to the main desk where two guards sat.

"Good morning," Bayer forced a smile, "I have a 9:30 appointment with Maya Humboldt. I'm Bayer Thompson."

"Good morning, Mr. Thompson, if you can just look into this little camera right here," the man pointed toward the small sphere attached to the top of his computer monitor. The camera snapped a picture, and the guard held out a tablet with an illuminated square, "Your thumbprint, Sir."

Bayer's stress levels shot through the roof, "I don't have my ID on me. But I have this thing the DMV gave me-"

"No worries, Mr. Thompson, this will suffice for a visitor's pass." The guard handed him a badge with his photo and instructed him where he needed to go for his meeting. While getting past the security desk was a mild achievement, it didn't do much to soften the rapid thudding of Bayer's pulse thrumming inside of his ears.

When Bayer stepped off the elevator, he was greeted by a short woman whose ponytail looked incredibly tight and her face even tighter. The scowl on her face screamed volumes, telling Bayer this wasn't going to end well.

"Good morning," Bayer smiled, making eye contact with an outstretched hand. "I'm Bayer Thompson."

"Good morning, Mr. Thompson," the woman's voice held a nasal inflection making him wonder if she was sick. He shook her hand anyway. "All I need is your ID to get you an access pass and-"

"I sent an email to Miss Humboldt yesterday explaining the situation regarding my identification. Can I use this visitor's pass?"

"I'm Miss Humboldt," the woman sneered, "And, no, you can't. If you'd checked your email this morning, you would have seen that I told you to come prepared with an alternative means of identification. You know, a passport or something. I cannot show you the server room to have you complete the necessary assessments required for this interview without giving you an access code. You cannot receive an access code without proper identification and clearance from our Intellectual Property Manager. Since you've neglected to come prepared for this interview, it's best to assume that there will be days you will be unprepared for this position. Thank you for coming in, Mr. Thompson, but at this time, we will decline to move forward in the hiring process. I wish you well on your employment search."

Bayer's anxiety shifted to anger quickly as he desperately wanted to get a word in with Miss Humboldt. She never gave him a chance, spinning on her heels and walking away without a second thought. She'd left Bayer in the elevator bank, with the only option being to head back down to the lobby and home.

He laughed to himself. "Doing the right thing ain't ever did shit for me."

6

"Two weeks," Holcomb mumbled under his breath, scrolling through an endless sea of recording files on his computer. "I can't believe it's been two weeks and nothing!"

"Yeah, normally, Jimbo has something for us by now. We can canvas the neighborhood again and see what pops up." Israel took a sip of his coffee while thumbing through a few sheets of paper in front of him.

Holcomb growled, slamming his hands against the desk, "That's not what I'm talking about! I don't care about some wannabe drug Scarface dealer. I've been combing through these files listening to every conversation that mentions Sinclair, and there's nothing here about Thompson."

Israel rolled his eyes, folding his arms across his chest, "What do you mean? I thought you were leaving that guy alone. We have other assignments given to us specifically that we need to work on for this task force. What's your thing with this Bayer guy? Don't tell me he's just some pawn to get to Sinclair. What did either of them do to you?!"

Holcomb closed his eyes, "None of that matters anymore. Just know that what I'm doing is for the greater good."

"Fine. It's obvious you're not going to let this go, so why don't you tell me what you got so far?"

"Nothing concrete, just that Sinclair sent Thompson to relay a message, and that's the last I heard of it."

Israel's furrowed brow preceded a soft scratch to the chin, "And what was this message?"

"I don't know I wasn't there," Holcomb

mumbled to himself.

"And what did Sinclair say exactly when he sent Thompson to relay a message? And who was the message sent to? How do we even know Thompson was the one to send this message?"

Holcomb's frustration bubbled up, "I don't know! I don't know! That's why I'm listening to these wires!"

"Exactly," Israel pointed at Holcomb, "You don't know what you're looking for, and you don't have shit on Thompson. For the love of God, let that man live his life. You're going to fuck up this multiagency investigation because of this vendetta that I'm starting to believe is against Thompson more than it is Sinclair. Tell me what's going on, Leon."

Holcomb was at a loss for words refusing to give Israel all of the information. He rose out of his chair, frustration and anger steaming from his collar, and shoved past his partner.

Israel stopped Detective Holcomb with a firm grasp to his shoulder, whispering, "Whatever it is you got against this Thompson guy, let it go. Whatever you think he's going to do with Sinclair, let it go. If that man violates his parole, you need to go through the proper channels and reach out to his PO if you want to know his exact whereabouts. You'd better not fuck this investigation up over some personal bullshit!"

Holcomb snatched his shoulder away from his partner's grasp. "I'm gonna do whatever the fuck I wanna do and make sure justice is served. Thompson didn't do enough time for me to forget every life taken because of his actions that night."

Holcomb's words gave Israel pause. He desperately wanted to know what drove Holcomb's obsession with the parolee, "So you have some affiliation with the Hungarian mobsters Thompson took out to help that stripper? Or was it the stripper? Tell me."

The vindictive detective's words were short and pushed through clenched teeth, "Bayer Thompson and Cesar Sinclair are going to pay for the lives they ended that night."

Israel stood there waiting for Holcomb to say more, but he didn't. Detective Holcomb stormed out of the office and the precinct without so much as another word to anyone.

*****

Olivia Sanders-Thompson sat across from her paroled ex-husband at a table overlooking the water with the Manhattan skyline just across the river. She held onto her beauty gloriously. However, the frown she wore aged her significantly every time Bayer looked at her. Beautiful skin with dark brown eyes to match her glorious and well-paid hourglass shape.

"I'm here," Bayer sighed with his hands folded

on the table, inches away from a hot cup of coffee.

"Why can't we go inside, Bayer?" Olivia whined with chattering teeth. "It's freezing out here."

"I know," Bayer smirked. The colder it was meant she wouldn't talk his ear off for no good goddamn reason. He wanted Olivia to get to the point, and nothing helped her do that better than the cold air nipping at her inadequately dressed ass. "You'd better hurry up then."

Olivia took a deep breath to blow the hot exhale into her un-gloved hands, rubbing them together vigorously in a poor attempt to warm them up. "Why you ain't come to see me since you been out, Bay?"

"I hate it when you call me that, and you know why. What do you want, Olivia?"

"I need three more in alimony," she rushed out.

That tipped Bayer's head back in boisterous

laughter, "Now, you know that ain't gonna happen. So tell me what you really want."

"I just told you," she sniffed back tears, "Malcolm lost his job, and I've been footing the bill. I'm only coming clean because I know you want to check to see if I'm lying. I'd only need the bump for a few months."

Bayer laughed even harder, letting a tear come down his cheek, "Damn, I needed that. You're fucking hilarious, Liv. Ain't no way in hell I'm giving you a dime more than required. Not to mention I'm unemployed. Where do you think this extra three grand a month is gonna come from?"

"The same account my alimony checks come from. Can't you tell them to up the monthly payout?"

Bayer pulled himself closer to the table, leaning in close enough for Olivia to strain as he vehemently uttered, "If you want an extra three grand a month to support you and your live-in domestic partner, I suggest you petition the court for that. I've done the right thing by you, and this is what I get? Two whole ass healthy adults asking me to pay their bills when I'm fresh out of prison, and they ain't had nothing but time to get their shit together. Olivia, please hear me very clearly when I say fuck you. Wait a minute, does Malcolm even know you're here?"

Olivia's eyes cut away as tears streamed down her cheeks, "He wants me to work!"

"So."

Olivia's head snapped back at him, furiously whipping her hair in front of her face, "I haven't worked since Cory took a breath on this planet, and you want me to try and get a job now?"

"Oh, cut the shit, Liv," Bayer spat, "You're not stupid. Or hell, you must be if you think I am. I ain't Malcolm. I know the kind of hustle that gets you out of bed in the morning. So you better get back on it because you smilin' in the wrong asshole's face if you think I'm footing the bill for you and your husband to take month-long vacations and live rent-free without having to lift a finger except to count my fucking money."

"Fine," she huffed, "I'll just call Mr. McKinley in the morning to start the proceedings."

"And get laughed right out of court. I'm calling your bluff, Liv. Ain't no petition being granted to a woman living with her husband for the past six years. I may have been in prison, but my PI wasn't. I have all of the documents I need to prove you two been living together, cohabitating, the lovely fucking couple. I'm tired of this shit. Just leave me alone, Olivia. For the sake of our son and the future where he wants both of his parents in the same room together, leave me the fuck alone. I won't touch the account now, but you two have a year before I petition the court to cease the payments. Take it or leave it, Liv."

"Bay, please," she begged. "If I ever meant anything to you-"

Bayer held his hand up to stop her as he got up from the table, "Cut that shit and save those tears for your next mark. I'm not even mad. I've always been the easiest to get money out of, but our son is grown with a family of his own. Don't you dare send him to ask me for money to give to you either! If I get the slightest whiff you're siphoning money out of him, fuck this nice guy shit, Liv, I'll gut you like a fucking fish. I did time already. I ain't got no problem going back over my son. You hear me?"

Olivia stared at Bayer with shock in her eyes. Fear and respect wouldn't let her say anything, so she nodded her head and watched him walk away.

Bayer Thompson was through. For everything he tried to do right, something happened to tell him he'd been doing shit the wrong way for as long back as he could remember. The only voice he could hear was Cory's as he walked away from the mother of his child. This isn't fair. You didn't do anything wrong.

Fuck doing the right thing. Bayer made up his mind that from that point on, he'd only do what was right … for him.

7

Detective Holcomb took three days of personal leave to follow a hunch, a fucking hunch. The same three guys he thought he intimidated from Staten Island hadn't made a single peep as to his warning message. He peeked inside the restaurant he trashed to see the mirror replaced. It was like he'd never been there.

"Why didn't they say anything?" The words frustrated him with every minute that passed. He continued to groan and gripe, "Why haven't they rained down chaos on Thomson and Sinclair?"

Pain radiated through his hands from the force of his fingernails digging into his palm. His clenched fists shook with silent rage as he watched the three men he'd surveilled that day from three weeks ago. Instead of letting his emotions get the better of him, he opted to return another day, keeping his off-duty surveillance a top priority.

Day after day, he came back to the restaurant, waiting for the goons to act. He didn't intrude on their dinners, not a single breakfast interrupted, nor a lunch disturbed. Detective Holcomb pursued three members of the Hungarian mafia, only knowing that Bayer Thompson killed two of their men nearly seven years ago under orders from Johnie Irish and Cesar Sinclair. At least, that's what he thought he knew.

The moonlit night was cold. The breeze whipped through the air whirring loudly, whistling just beneath the stars. Holcomb pulled at his closed jacket, willing warmth into his body as the chattering of his frigid scowl gave him the perfect soundtrack to his evening.

Gloved hands didn't help.

The extra thick sweater underneath his hoodie and coat didn't help.

The extra pair of socks and thermal underwear with his combat boots didn't help.

The temperature dropped mercilessly, but Holcomb's resolve was stronger than any New York winter night. The shadows held him for three, four, five hours in an alley behind a restaurant where three men sat day in and day out. He'd take a few quiet steps and watched them through cracks in the door before returning to his spot in the alley to wait for the perfect time.

He tried his best to remain inconspicuous, refusing to let his ego break down the front door seeking answers to the myriad of questions circling his mind. No … Holcomb found plenty of time to watch three Hungarian mobsters throughout their day and drummed up the perfect plan. Tonight was the night he'd execute it, and this incident would be the catalyst to his self-serving justice.

Glancing at his watch, Holcomb noted the time.

"12:45." He muttered to himself. "Soon, very soon."

Precisely 15 minutes later, three men exited the restaurant to take their cigarette break at one in the morning. They didn't see the detective guarded in the shadows. It was the third night in a row they didn't see him. They smoked their cigarettes.

Holcomb made his presence known by clearing his throat. The shortest of the trio flicked his cigarette at the detective's feet. "Aye, who are you, and what the fuck do you want?"

"I wanna talk to your boss, and you're gonna tell me how to find him," Holcomb growled.

"You're barking up the wrong tree," the short one chuckled, "I ain't got no boss, Boss."

"Yeah, you do, and he knows me well. Getting put away for killing y'all homies ain't did shit but give me time, and now I got the opportunity."

"What the fuck are ya yapping about? Get to the point!" the man replied.

Holcomb didn't wait another second before pulling out his gun fitted with a silencer. The first bullet he squeezed out hit the shortest one square between the eyes. The second bullet moved just as quickly, taking out the man to the left of the short one, while the third bullet he purposely put in the knee of the remaining gentleman.

Holcomb rushed toward the man before he had a chance to scream any louder. Muffling his impending wails of pain with his gloved hand, Holcomb held the muzzle of his gun to the man's temple. "I ain't gonna kill you, but this is the last time I'm gonna give you this message. Tell Biro Barnabas that I'm looking for him, that I'm coming for him, and that nothing's going to stop Bayer from putting him and everyone working for him six feet under. I've done enough time over that asshole, and I'm prepared to do more or die trying."

Holcomb smashed the butt of his gun against the man's head, knocking him unconscious with the hopes he'd remember the message clearly when he came out of it. The vindictive detective walked out of the alley and turned his face side to side before walking down the street and turning the corner.

There wasn't an SUV waiting for him this time. He'd returned that to the impound lot already, opting to keep his vigilante surveillance on foot. Sweat poured from his scalp making his hat even colder. His hands trembled as the vacant stares of his victims haunted him immediately. It didn't matter to Holcomb. He had their rap sheets. He knew every crime they'd been booked for and every indictment that never stuck. They deserved everything he did to them.

It was the right thing to do to get the justice that needed to be served. However, being the swift hand of justice made Holcomb sick. He doubled over at the waist with his hands on his knees, gasping in the cold night air. His chest tightened with every inhale as pain ripped through him. Anxiety, fear, and anger for what he'd done tore at his fragile conscience.

"They're the bad guys. I didn't do anything wrong. I'm the cop. I'm doing the right thing."

Holcomb muttered the words over and over again to himself. The further he moved away from the restaurant, the more he relaxed. He continued to push himself away from the scene of his double homicide and aggravated assault. The quiver in his bottom lip allowed doubt to seep in, but only for a moment.

The yelling of angered men and screeching

sirens blaring through the wee hours of the morning pulled Detective Holcomb out of his emotions and back into reality. He had to get the hell out of there. Shoving his hands in his pockets, he kept walking until he eventually found his way home. Sleep found him sooner than he thought, and so did the morning.

A few hours later, sometime after the sun met the sky, Holcomb dragged himself into work. Murder had sapped his energy. Israel's face said everything before his words echoed around the room, "You look like shit, Leon."

"Didn't know looking like the King of England was a requirement," Holcomb sniped at his partner.

The irritable detective fought the urge to let his face hit the desk, gripping his coffee mug like a life preserver. The eardrum piercing drag of the porcelain cup across the top of the desk made Israel's shoulders hunch and his face twist in agony. The more it made Israel uncomfortable, the better it made Holcomb feel. He dragged the mug even slower before pulling it up to his mouth, where he slurped the hot caffeine slowly.

"It's not, but coming into work looking like you've walked the entire island of Manhattan barefoot while tripping acid doesn't scream I'm here to serve and protect. What the hell is going on with you, bro?"

Holcomb sniffed like he wanted to cry, "I don't know. I don't know. Just a lot on my mind, I guess."

"Why don't you take the rest of the week off? I'll make sure your shift is covered. I can pull Grady in on this new case until you're back in shape to do actual police work."

"Huh? What case?" Holcomb felt the fog lifting.

"Last night," Israel scrolled through the screen

on his phone, "The one and only son of Biro Barnabas, found behind some restaurant with his bodyguard. Both killed. Execution style. PD wasn't on the scene until early this morning."

"How early?" Holcomb asked.

"I don't know, about five or six. The scene had been tampered with, of course. We're guessing Barnabas had his boys remove weapons or anything else that could incriminate him. We have a meeting at ten with three other departments to pool resources and keep a lid on this powder keg."

"Huh?" Holcomb's confusion only annoyed Israel more.

"No one, and I mean no one, on the street knew Alexander Valenti was the son of Biro Barnabas. 'This has to be a major player' is what people are thinking. The police chief himself wants this guy found and brought in so they can protect him from Barnabas. We want a suspect in custody, so Barnabas doesn't start dropping bodies on us either. We can't have the grieving father, the eastern point man for the Hungarian mafia, on a bloody rampage. We need to solve this quickly and quietly on top of task force duties. It's a priority, but again, you look like dog shit ran over twice. Go home and get some sleep. Come in on Monday. Sober, perhaps? Rested, at least, and ready to work."

"Fuck you, Jessup. Are you sure that little pissant was Barnabas' son? And it was just him and the bodyguard found? No other person, maybe there was a third, and they left or something."

"Yes, I'm sure. NYPD was notified by someone close to him. A warning of sorts to let us know that a can of kerosene is about to be poured all over this dumpster fire. If there was a third person, then Barnabas probably has them by now. That's why they're throwing this meeting together. It's all hands on deck."

"Well, if it's all hands on deck, then I'm staying. I'm going to mix some Jack with my coffee to get my head out of my ass and into this case. I could use the distraction, honestly."

"It's whatever you wanna do. I'm no shrink, but I think you should take a few more days off. Take them now before you become obsessed with this case too."

"I'll be fine," Holcomb lied, but he wouldn't be fine. He put his head down as he fought to keep his coffee from coming back up.

There hadn't been any doubt in his mind the men he killed the night before were mere foot soldiers. The son of the head of the entire organization is not supposed to be smoking cigarettes in an alley at one in the morning. He was fucked. He didn't know how to fix it, so he did the only thing he knew how. Detective Holcomb decided to bury himself in the case if only to stay close enough to the investigation and keep himself off the chopping block.

8

"Hey, Cory," Bayer spoke into the phone with frustration. "I'm trying to get a hold of Claire to see if she needs anything from the store before I head home. You don't seem to be answering either. I guess I'll just grab some wings or something. Let me know if you guys want anything."

Bayer disconnected the call to Cory's voicemail with dread in his heart. Even when Cory was busy, he'd respond with a text or something. He didn't want to jump to conclusions. The craziness of the cops scrambling all over the city from that double homicide a few nights ago left him on edge. Bayer grabbed something to eat before making his way home. He shoved a hand deeper in his pocket, tucking his takeout closer to his body as he trekked through the evening, anxious to sit down and relax.

"You're trippin, man," Bayer mumbled to himself. He tried to calm the uneasiness plaguing his heart. Every deep breath swept through his body with agony and tightness he couldn't shake. Still, he managed to make his way home.

The street was too quiet. It all seemed out of place. Every step Bayer took toward his son's home forced his heart to thump harder against his chest. The soft thrumming of its rapid beat inside of his ears pushed him to pick up his pace. By the time he reached the driveway, it had dawned on him what was wrong. Cory's car was in front of Claire's truck at an angle that didn't make sense.

Bayer's hand trembled, stretching it out to touch the hood of his son's car. The coldness said it had been sitting for a while. It looked like Cory pulled into the driveway in a hurry, slanted, almost pressed against Claire's truck with the keys still in the ignition. Bayer's adrenaline sent the bag of food to the ground, pushing his fears to the side and his body toward the front door. The door's lock sat at a crooked angle like it'd been pried out of place.

"CLAIRE!" Bayer's voice boomed through the cold house. The muffled screams of his daughter-in-law broke his heart as he flew down the hallway toward the kitchen. He didn't think to search the house for whoever had broken in. The silence around him, outside of Claire, told him the perpetrators were no longer in the house.

"Claire?" His voice shook, cracking as he prepared himself for the worst.

Claire sat bound to a chair. Her ankles were tied to the legs, with her wrists bound behind the back of the seat. She was blindfolded with a shred of torn cloth and a similar piece tied around her mouth, keeping her cries muffled and inaudible to the world. The pool of blood resting under her began to stick around the edges.

The first thing he did was remove her blindfold. Claire's right eye swelled, and both were puffy from the tears she'd been shedding. Taking off the gag gave him a better look at her face. She'd been knocked around pretty good. Her lips quivered as she released heart-wrenching sobs into Bayer's hands.

"What the hell happened here? Claire, where are you hurt?" He hesitated to touch her as he desperately scanned to find the wound causing the pool of blood. The color drained from her beautiful deep brown skin as sweat beaded down her face, mixing with her tears. Her eyes drooped; she was on the verge of passing out. Bayer went to remove the restraints on her hands and feet when he saw it. A bullet hole through her thigh blew out the bottom of the chair.

None of this made sense.

The moment he released her legs, she let out a sigh of relief. Her arms were too weak to wrap around his neck as Bayer cradled her in his arms. Tears flowed from his eyes as he ran to Cory's car with Claire barely coherent. He didn't know how long she'd been tied up, and he'd begun to panic thinking about his son. Cory would have never let this happen to her.

He pulled out his phone, dialing the one person who could help him.

"Mr. Thompson, is everything alright? Your check-in is tomorrow, and I call you," Genevieve Parsons stated.

"I'm sorry, but I need your help. Someone broke into Cory's house tonight."

"Oh my God! Is he alright? What about your daughter-in-law?"

Bayer sniffed back tears, "She's been shot. She took a few blows to the face. I don't have any idea where Cory is. I can't risk waiting for 911 to get here, so I'm bringing her in myself. I'm taking her to Bailey Memorial. Can you call the cops and let them know where I'm going to be and that they can question me there?"

"Bayer," Genevieve's professionalism slipped away, "I don't think that's a good idea. Call your lawyer and have him meet you at the hospital before you talk to the police. If they lock you up for this-"

"Gen, I swear I didn't do this. I love my son and his wife. I'd never do anything to hurt them."

"Bayer, I know, but cops are less likely to put cuffs on you with your lawyer there. If Detective Holcomb shows up, you're going to need your lawyer. Bayer, please, just do what I'm telling you. Call him now and have him meet you there. I'll go to your house and wait for the cops to show up."

"Wow. I thought you'd help me, but I had no

idea you'd do this much."

"I already told you why I do this. It's for guys like you who get the short end of the stick when all they want to do is the right thing. I won't let the system take another man like you off the street without a fight. I'll call you when I get to Cory's house. Bayer?"

"Yeah?"

"Do you think that Cory?" her voice trailed off.

"Not a chance in hell my son did this to his wife. She was tied to a chair with a bullet hole through her thigh. I need to find him. I don't even know where to start. I keep calling his phone, but he's not picking up."

"Okay, one thing at a time. Get Claire taken care of, and we'll worry about Cory next."

Genevieve disconnected the call letting Bayer call his lawyer. By the time he reached the hospital, Claire was barely coherent, and his lawyer was already standing there in jeans and a t-shirt.

Martin Sanchez couldn't hide the worried expression behind his eyes as Bayer delicately scooped Claire from the passenger side of the car. When the hospital's personnel tried to take her out of his arms, she panicked, wrapping her arms around his neck and her eyes shot open.

"They took him," she whispered to Bayer, "A son for a son."

Before he could ask her anything else, she passed out again. He laid her on the gurney letting the doctors and nurses do their job.

"What did she say?" Martin asked, walking toward Bayer.

"Nothing. She didn't tell me anything," he lied. He'd have to decipher Claire's words another time.

"I just don't understand why this is happening."

"Come on," Martin nudged Bayer toward the ER waiting room, "Tell me what's going on."

Bayer laid everything on him from that night to his run-in with Detective Holcomb, which led Genevieve to suggest he call him there. Martin sat in silence, absorbing every detail until two officers approached them.

"Are you here with the victim from 30-28 Maple Drive? A Claire Thompson with a gunshot wound to the right thigh?" One of the uniformed officers asked.

Martin stood up immediately, "We are here with her. This is my client, Bayer Thompson. You two are awfully quick. Gunshot wounds usually take a few hours before PD shows up."

The officer glimmered, "Will you two come with us, please?"

There wasn't any explanation of anything else as the officer led them to an empty conference room somewhere beyond the halls, where they waited for updates on Claire's condition. Martin and Bayer sat down, waiting to see how the police would pin this on his client. They didn't have to wait long as one of the officers who stepped inside loosened his tie and removed his hat.

"Don't say anything!" The officer instructed Martin and Bayer. "I'm here on behalf of an interested party who knows the whereabouts of Mr. Thompson's son. You're to meet with this interested person tomorrow at 6 am. Do not tell NYPD. Do not tell the FBI or any other agency, or your son's life will be in further jeopardy. Here."

The officer, well, the man in an officer's uniform, slid a business card across the table. "Show up to the address alone. No police. The whereabouts of your son will be revealed to you, along with other pertinent information. The only request is that you keep this scenario as a home invasion gone wrong. Is that clear?"

"Yes!" Bayer snatched the card, nodding his head up and down vigorously. He didn't have time to ask any questions as the officer left the room.

By the time the real police showed up, he'd already made up his mind to head to the appointment alone. They asked a bunch of questions and were able to verify Bayer's alibi with his receipt and security footage from the fast food place. He'd told them that Cory hadn't gotten home yet and that his phone probably died. When the officers left, he found Genevieve waiting for him, surrounded by patients who hadn't been shot during a kidnapping.

"Officer Parsons," Martin tipped his head to her.

She smiled, getting out of her seat with warmth in her eyes. "Thank you, Mr. Sanchez."

"You're very welcome," Martin nodded, "If I can have a word with my client, please."

Bayer watched Genevieve excuse herself to get some coffee before turning to Martin. "What's on your mind?"

"I can't help but think that tomorrow's meeting is a setup. I didn't want to say anything in front of your parole officer. She seems to care about you a lot. I don't need to tell you how to handle her, do I?"

"No," Bayer growled, "She's handled that on her own just fine. About tomorrow, you don't have to worry about that either. I'm going to that meeting. I don't care if it's a setup or not. I need to do this for Cory."

"The men you're dealing with," Martin sighed, rubbing the bridge of his nose, "These are not men who can be bargained or reasoned with. You're playing a dangerous game if you head into that meeting on your own."

"Well, I can't show up with cops on my tail either. I can't have anything jeopardizing Cory's return. Just stick with me. Isn't that what your retainer is for? Sticking with me?"

"It is," Martin scowled a bit before his shoulders sunk, relenting to Bayer's request. "Fine, if you must do this on your own, I insist on you protecting yourself."

"Do you know what you're suggesting?" Bayer asked him.

"I'm simply stating, as your attorney, that if you enter into a space with unsavory individuals that you protect yourself within the means of the law and the rights provided to you as a parolee under the supervision of New York State." Martin stopped Bayer with a stiff hand to his bicep, "And as someone who knows every inch and detail of your case, and the kind of man you're willing to become to protect yourself and your family, I am telling you not to go into that meeting without a fucking semi-auto. Bayer, I know how you feel about your son, but I also know how you feel about doing the right thing. Please, Bayer, do the right thing."

"And what's that?!" Bayer snapped. He grabbed Martin by the collar, yanking him so close to his face he could see the beads of spit that landed on his cheek with every word he spoke, "Calling the cops in to fuck up getting my son back!? I am tired of doing the right fucking thing all of the time and getting nothing for it in return! From here on out, I'm doing things my way. The only thing you need to do is keep me out of fucking jail! Believe me; I'm going to make your job as easy as possible!"

9

Bayer decided to be the man he'd become over the past six years, locked away in a cell. There were things he'd done. Horrors he survived in a maximum-security prison that he'd never dream of burdening his family with. Bayer knew he never worked for Cesar Sinclair, it only took one person to believe he did, and his life was ruined from the mere implication.

Thoughts droned on.

Quiet breaths synced with the clicks of his steps echoing down the hospital halls. Even with the hustle and busy work of the floor, he felt the stillness in the silence until he reached the waiting area. Bayer locked eyes with Genevieve, motioning his head toward the door, letting her know he was leaving. She followed him out of the hospital waiting room, catching up to him in the parking lot.

"How is she?" Genevieve asked.

Bayer turned to her with a peculiar look in his eyes before it registered what she'd asked him, "Um, she's been shot. I can't say anything more than that. I do want to thank you for handling the police that came to my son's house. I have things that I need to do to protect my family."

"Bayer," her voice trembled with her fingers just as shaky as her tone when she touched him. Bayer flinched, pulling away from her grasp. She swallowed before coiling her fingers into fists held against her thighs. "Bayer, please don't do whatever it is you're thinking about doing."

"What is it that you think I'm about to do?"

"I don't know," Genevieve shrugged, shaking her head from side to side. "I don't know, but I see the look in your eyes. Your energy is different."

"Why shouldn't I be different?!" He growled. "My son is missing! Someone broke into my kid's house, knocked my daughter around before putting a bullet in her leg. She's in that hospital, most likely paying for something my past caused. But, here you are, wanting me to be the same man who checks in with you."

Bayer tipped his head down, drawing her tear-welled eyes into his gaze, waiting for a reaction, but she turned away, avoiding his glare. He slid his finger under her chin, turning her face back to him. He even leaned his forehead against hers, inhaling her scent slowly.

"Bayer," she whispered with her lip quivering. "I just don't want you getting put back in that cage. Please don't do anything to-"

He stopped her words with the softest kiss on her lips. Before she could push him away, Bayer took a step back and let his lips move to her forehead, "I'm never going back inside. You want me to bend over backward to follow these laws, these rules that keep me shackled and fucking muzzled like a damn dog! Fuck all of that. Thank you for what you did tonight. Thank you for making me get Martin down here. I want you to go home and don't worry about me."

"Okay," she wiped a tear off her cheek. "Bayer, just … just be careful."

"I'm going to come to your office sometime this week, and I need you to do what I ask you, okay?"

"What does that mean?" Genevieve asked him.

"That means I need to figure some things out and how to keep you out of the shit storm that's coming. Okay?"

Bayer waited for Genevieve to ask more questions, but she didn't. She let him leave the parking lot without another warning to heed nor word to listen to. He made his way to the place his son called home with a heaviness in his heart he knew would never let him sleep.

Instead, Bayer roamed through the darkness, running his fingertips along the walls and wondering if the men who took his son touched the same places. The animal caged inside of him had only been set free a time or two. He hated who he had to become within the confines of prison. Now, he sees the violence he survived would serve another purpose.

By the time the sun rose, Bayer traced the lines in his face trying to read into his future. His imagination showed him nothing but bloodshed on a desperate search to bring his son home. Cory was a good man. Neither of them deserved what happened. Their only fault was allowing him to stay there. So he stood in their home without a single scratch to his body, seething and guilt-ridden over an event he knew was meant for him. However, Bayer refused to shed any more tears. He fastened his resolve that if the world was going to treat him like he worked for Cesar Sinclair, he would use it to his advantage. With that, he took off into the morning.

Another office building in Midtown Manhattan housed the address given to him the night before. There wasn't anyone in the lobby except for a large security guard dressed in swat gear. His expression didn't sway from the 'Don't Fuck Wit Me' scrawled across his face.

"Bayer Thompson, I have an appointment this morning."

The security guard eyed Bayer from head to toe before motioning for him to step over a thick black line next to the desk. After Bayer could see behind the desk, a monitor showed an x-ray machine of sorts. He couldn't stop his eyes from scanning the room for the technology, but all he managed to spot was a thick line blending seamlessly into the wall.

"First elevator on your right. You're going to the eighth floor," the guard told him.

"Aren't you going to ask me for an ID or something?"

"No."

Bayer nodded and proceeded with caution as he wondered who'd called this meeting with him. All of the movies would have you believe kidnappers call with a disguised voice asking for a ransom, but this didn't have that feeling to it. He never imagined who would have pertinent information to his son's abduction. Still, when the elevator doors opened, seeing Cesar Sinclair himself nearly knocked him over.

Sinclair wasn't a tall man. He didn't ooze danger as the media would have you believe. He looked the part of a sophisticated and confident businessman. Black hair peppered with strands of grey and slicked back kept his look neat with sophistication. There weren't muscles to be seen, but something about his presence didn't diminish the air of danger living inside of the kingpin. He didn't smile at Bayer but held out his hand to greet him.

"Mornin' Mr. Thompson," Sinclair greeted Bayer, "I hate that it's under these circumstances that I have to bring you into our office, but neither I nor my partner could sit on the sidelines while this catastrophe unfolded on your doorstep. Please, follow me."

Bayer didn't speak a word to the man known only for his infamy and heinous crimes. While none of it was proven, he knew better than to test the waters. The office was plain, bland, and screamed boredom.

"Have a seat, Mr. Thompson." Sinclair waved his hand in front of the empty chair.

"No large desk? And where's your partner?" Bayer surveyed the room.

"No. No large desk. No penthouse. Nothing fancy. Nothing that draws attention," he grinned with an air of mystery. "Johnie doesn't come in until later. It's just us here. Please have a seat."

Bayer finally sat down to Sinclair's appeasement. "So what catastrophe is unfolding? And do you know where my son is? Is he hurt?"

Sinclair served up his explanation for current events, "You, my unexpected ally, have helped me twice in my life without you ever being aware of it. The second time cost you six months in the SHU and a few broken bones. I thought by getting you released early; I'd paid my debt."

"What?" Bayer's confusion bordered on anger.

"Take it easy. I just pushed your lawyer and a few others working on your parole to work a little harder." It's all Sinclair would ever say about his parole being granted before Bayer served out his minimum.

"I did what I had to do to stay alive. That guy attacked me. He was going to kill me. I didn't have a choice," Bayer admitted in a low tone. He desperately tried to stop the memories of the incident from replaying in his mind.

"That guy thought you worked for me," Sinclair revealed.

"What else is fucking new?" Bayer growled under his breath.

Sinclair huffed out his reply. "You taking him out in self-defense helped me far more than you could ever imagine. Seeing as I've paid men to do less, I thought it only right to toss you a bone."

"What does any of this have to do with my son? The guy, who looked a lot like a cop, who told me to come here, said I'd be given his location and other pertinent information."

"You, Bayer Thompson, have a vigilante cop on your hands who thinks he is above the shield. I was hauled out of my peaceful sleep because Alexander Valenti was murdered a few days ago. Very few people knew he was the son of Biro Barnabas. Biro Barnabas is a man of principle like yourself but with a much higher body count. I'm telling you this because the man who killed Alexander made it a point to tell the victim he left behind that you and I were behind the hit."

Bayer's fingers gripped his scalp as if to tear it from his skull, "You are becoming the bane of my existence, Sinclair. What do I need to do to convince the world I don't work for you?"

"You don't need to do anything. Anyone who can see knows you don't, but that brings me to the events that unfolded that night. This cop who's got a hardon for you killed that kid and his bodyguard. I don't think he knew he was inciting a war, but we can't have that happen. This city, my organization, the Hungarian outfit, no one can afford the onslaught of bloodshed. When I heard Barnabas was moving through the city like a damn plague, a son for a son, I tried to get to you, but it was too late. They'd already taken him.

I can't promise what kind of condition he's in, but I know he's alive. His location will be sent to you after you leave this building, but I wanted to give you this information face to face with a warning…Do not kill or attack Biro. That is wrath your family will never be free of. Not a single generation moving forward will go untouched. It took him two days to track you and your family down. If you seek vengeance, I suggest you take the proper measures to ensure that the cop is brought to justice. Do the right thing."

"I'm not interested in playing the concerned citizen; I just want my son and to be done with all of you. Why can't I just live my life in peace?"

Bayer asked no one.

"Peace is only granted to the dead. Do what you want after you leave here. Just don't do anything that will bleed all over my doorstep. You have my sincerest apologies for the way my name has tainted your life, Mr. Thompson. I just want to do the right thing by you and make sure your son gets to come home."

The words grated on Bayer's nerves, but what else could he do? It wasn't the guy's fault people connected them. Only one thing was certain, Bayer had to stop doing unintentional favors for criminals if he had any chance of getting his life under control. He thanked the man and left the building. Just as he promised, a text came through to his phone with an address with precise instructions to come alone.

10

Bayer expected to arrive at some abandoned warehouse, wet with rats scurrying around. However, shock overtook him as he stepped out of a cab and into a ritzy neighborhood in Brooklyn. He walked toward a glass door that held a number etched onto the pane. Nothing made the building stand out from the attached Brownstone walk-ups trailing down the street. After ringing the bell, a voice shouted through a speaker, "Take off your jacket and lift your shirt. Turn around in a complete circle, slowly."

Bayer did as he was instructed. After, a loud buzzer sounded with the clicking of the lock moving out of place. He pushed his way into the building's entryway to be greeted by another door. This one didn't allow people to peek inside. It buzzed open only after the first one shut and locked.

Bayer hadn't prepared himself for what was behind that door, but pristine white walls weren't anywhere on his radar. The place smelled sterile. Not an ounce of dust to be seen nor a single stain to stand out. There looked to be an empty waiting room to his left and a set of stairs to his right.

Directly in front of him was a long hallway of sharp white walls and closed doors. He took a few steps down the hall when a man standing at a staggering 6'5" with oily black hair and a thick handlebar mustache appeared at the end of the corridor. He held two palms in the air for Bayer to stop walking. Then the tall man snapped his fingers. Another man seemed to appear out of thin air to search Bayer's body, but more likely, he came out of the waiting area he'd just walked by.

"Mr. Thompson." The tall man in charge spoke gruffly and held his hand out, "I am Biro Barnabas.

May I ask you to have a seat and have a discussion with me, yes?"

"I don't have much of a choice if I want to walk out of here with my boy, do I?"

"Life is full of choices, Mr. Thompson. Your choices, whether intentional or not, have yielded consequences that have brought you to this moment. What you choose to do after you leave here will yield another set of consequences, so I think you should talk to me first."

Bayer nodded and followed the man into a small room with nothing but a table, two chairs, and a tablet sitting on top of it. He pulled a chair out to sit down, turning its back to a corner so he could see anyone coming into the room. He kept silent, waiting for the man to speak.

"I am Biro. I am a very dangerous man to play games with. Someone stole my son's life, and without seeking the truth from all angles, I reacted prematurely. Your son is alive, but he's beaten badly; not in very good shape at all."

"I'm sure it's because you shot his wife," Bayer snapped.

"Yes, your son and his wife had no idea what they were up against, but still, they fought a valiant fight. It was only after we put a bullet in her leg that he came without struggle. We've been tending to his injuries here. It will take some time for the bruising to go down, but he will be fine. The girl's wounds aren't life-threatening. She will heal as well."

Bayer only heard the subtle shifting of his molars grinding against one another as he heeded Sinclair's warning. "Why shouldn't I call the police on you?"

"Because that doesn't help anyone, and I am in an excellent position to help you. Let me repay you and your family for the unintentional treachery

I've unleashed."

Biro didn't waste his words as he gave Bayer a folder and turned on the tablet. He pulled an envelope from a back pocket and slid it across the table to Bayer with his words low, "Before you refuse the money think about this. Neither your son nor daughter-in-law will be able to work for a few weeks, which may force them out of their employment. They need the money. Please give it to them. It's only 300,000 dollars, but that's all I could scrape together since last night."

A pang of guilt and envy hit Bayer like a ton of bricks that the man before him could scrape up 300 grand in a few hours. He'd taken an entire year to save half of that. Another subtle dig at his pride and ego to do the right thing. Bayer reached for the envelope, "I'll discuss it with them, but in case they refuse it, where do I return it?"

"Don't," Barnabas stated. "You're a smart man. Whatever you do, at least pay the taxes on it. If you need more, reach out to this number with a final amount, and it will be sent to you. But, something tells me this will be the last time we speak on this money."

Bayer knew that as well. He shifted the conversation, asking Barnabas, "When do I get to see my son?"

"I'm going to take you to see him in a few minutes, but let's discuss the contents of that folder and the files on the tablet. Hit the play button."

Bayer let out a sigh as he narrowed his gaze onto the small screen in front of him. The footage was crystal clear even in the darkness. A black guy executed two men in an alley. However, the face of the killer wasn't visible from the angle of this particular video. Bayer watched it a few more times before looking to Biro, waiting for an explanation.

"Play the next video," Biro instructed him.

Bayer did as he was told, touching the file next to the last video. This piece of footage showed something that shook Bayer to his core. He began to vibrate with anger as he watched Detective Holcomb's face come into view.

"I'm gonna fuckin kill him," he snarled.

"Don't," Biro warned, "The last thing any of us need is a dead cop in the city. I've done enough to get them riled up. He needs to pay for his treachery, but it cannot be by my hand."

"Leave him to me," Bayer said with certainty. "Now, take me to my son."

"I intend to do just that. The folder I gave you is all of the information I have available for the officer. I've uploaded the videos, all of them, to a cloud drive. The password and link are in the folder with the rest of it. Do what you will with that information. As for your son, I will warn you that he doesn't look good, but he receives the best care I can offer. You have my sincerest apologies for the misunderstanding."

Bayer was at a loss for words with the Hungarian mob boss. He elected not to say anything at all. Instead, he braced himself to see his son. Biro stood up from the table, and Bayer did the same. He pocketed the envelope full of cash and folded the file until he could hide it discreetly before following Biro to another room.

The soft beeping of machines monitoring Cory's vital signs broke Bayer's heart, and the sight before him did nothing to ease his agony. His boy, his law-abiding son, laid in a bed hooked up to several machines with his arm in a cast and a bandage around his head. There was a doctor and a nurse in the room tending to him as Bayer and Biro entered.

The doctor didn't bother to look up as he spoke while reading pages off of a clipboard, "Biro, he's going to be fine. The three broken ribs will heal in a few weeks, and the same goes for the radius. We'll keep him on pain meds, and he should be stable enough to move within a few hours."

Biro spoke with compassion to the doctor, "This is the young man's father. Please take his contact information so that we may let him know when and where we're going to move him."

Bayer sucked in a breath through clenched teeth, "He doesn't get to come home tonight?"

"No," the doctor peered up from his clipboard, "That's not the best thing for his recovery."

Biro turned to Bayer and whispered to him, "Your son and his wife will be moved into a private suite at Bailey Memorial. I will cover the costs of their hospital stay. It's the least I can do, especially for keeping this quiet."

"How do you know I'm going to keep this quiet?" Bayer grimaced. Every fiber in his body wanted revenge, but he knew it wasn't wholly Biro's fault. Holcomb opened up Pandora's box onto this city without any regard, and Holcomb would pay for his dangerous behavior.

Biro smirked a devilish grin, "You and I both know that you do not have the army to stand by you should you decide to go public with what's going on here. Besides, I am more than willing to pay for my mistakes and to offer my apologies. Kiss your son, Mr. Thompson, and thank Johnie Irish that he's still alive. This day could have very well begun with you looking for a burial plot. Do not mistake this remorseful demeanor for anything less than common courtesy. You got swept up in something due to no fault of your own. I only wish that you direct your karmic retribution to the person who let me out of my cage."

Bayer agreed with the man, even though he didn't want to admit it. So he left the nondescript brownstone with a file of information to review and his son healing from injuries he couldn't prevent. His mind drifted to his daughter in the hospital, nursing a bullet wound, another casualty from a war of which he's not on either side. So much chaos over a vendetta he had nothing to do with, and yet the criminals around him have proven to be more honorable than the policeman who started it.

At least with Biro footing the bill, Bayer knew his son and daughter would get the treatment they needed. A man willing to pay for what he'd done seemed commendable even if the criminal's gesture served a greater purpose than the minor one Bayer needed fulfilling. He set his mind at ease for the welfare of his family and focused on the tasks ahead of him, with Holcomb at the top of his list.

Bayer soaked in the sun, its brightness weighing on him differently with the knowledge that his family was okay for now. Holcomb would pay with his life for unleashing a different kind of monster he swore he'd leave in prison.

What Bayer truly needed was time. Time to think and devise the best revenge for a man who refused to leave him alone. As he plotted and schemed, every step taken away from his son's bedside hardened the beast baring its teeth, begging to be sicced on a target emblazoned into his memory. And still, patience washed over him like the warmth of the early afternoon.

Bayer chose to wait. He made his way to the corner in hopes of catching a taxi away from the block that housed a brownstone where his injured son recuperated. Just as he reached the intersection, an old lady dropped her grocery bag. Out of pure force of habit, Bayer rushed to her aid, stooping down to pick up the items spilling out onto the pavement. For his trouble, the woman's heavy pocketbook met the back of his head with a heavy thud.

"Don't you touch my things!" The older woman shouted. "I can do it myself."

Bayer raised his hands to the sky as he backed away, shaking his head and mumbling, "This nice guy shit really doesn't pay."

11

Claire shifted in her hospital bed, painfully uncomfortable with her leg lifted in a contraption she could have sworn she'd seen in a horror film. While they didn't drill any rods through her thigh, she could see the blood seeping into the bandages wrapped around her leg. Her eyes watered as she wished her husband were there, but at this point, she didn't even know if Cory was still alive.

Fear continued to ravage her mind as her eyes darted around the lonely hospital room. It was bigger than the first one they'd put her in, and even though there was room for another bed, she had it all to herself. Silence broadcasted from the TV hoisted in the corner, hanging from the ceiling. It didn't drive her to search for the remote to turn it on. She wanted answers. She wanted to know what the hell was going on.

A few soft raps on the door gave Claire pause. She wondered if whoever broke into their home came to see her in the hospital. Did they know where she was?

The doctor entering her room with a clipboard in her hands and a gentleman behind her eased her anxiety. The gleam of the light reflecting off of his badge made her even more comfortable.

"Good evening, Mrs. Thompson. I'm Dr. Ellie Azzarah, but you may call me Ellie, and this is Detective Holcomb. He just wants to ask you a few questions about how you ended up here. First, tell me, how are you feeling?"

Claire spoke softly, her throat irritated and voice raspy, "I feel like shit. Where's Cory? Uh, my husband? Is he here? I mean, in the hospital? He'd never leave me here alone."

"That's why I'm here," Holcomb spoke up but was immediately silenced by the doctor with a hand up to her shoulder to keep him back.

"Yes, you're going to be uncomfortable and in some pain for a few days. The good news is that the bullet went in and out, but it did nick your femur. No worries, we cleaned it all up, and the bone will heal fine on its own. There weren't any fractures or serious breaks to it, and the bullet spared your major blood vessels. So essentially, you're just healing from a flesh wound, and the stitches will dissolve in a week or so."

"Okay," Claire managed to squeak out.

"As far as your husband goes," Ellie's cheerful face shifted, "We've gotten word that he's on his way and is coming into this room with you. I don't have any updates on his condition as of right now."

"How long have I been here?" Claire asked.

"Two days," she told her. "You did lose a bit of blood, so you're going to be out of it. If you're not up to it, I can have this officer come back later."

"But-" Holcomb began to protest and was met with the same hand as before to keep him quiet.

"She's not under arrest, so she doesn't have to speak to you. My patient's care is my primary focus. If there's a crime to solve, you can wait until she's discharged," Ellie told Holcomb with certainty.

"It's okay," Claire said to the doctor. She shifted again as Ellie left the room and Holcomb approached her bedside.

"Can you tell me what happened?" Holcomb said with a stern voice, but something seemed off to Claire. He kept looking over his shoulder, glancing at the door like someone was going to burst in at any moment.

Flashes of the night attacked her, making her

relive it all over again. She closed her eyes, wishing for that fear to go away, but it stayed as she stammered through her recollection, "Um, I came home and was on the phone with Cory. I set my things down and moved to the kitchen, where I wanted to get dinner started. The back door looked busted, and before I could do anything about it, somebody hit me on the back of the head. I tried to run, but they came through the front too. I remember fighting as hard as I could, and finally, Cory came. He tried…"

Her voice drifted as the tears poured from her eyes. Claire's hands trembled in her lap, so she grabbed one hand with the other to ease the adrenaline, rage, and anxiety pumping all over her body.

"He tried to save me. He wouldn't stop fighting. Someone punched me in the face and knocked me out. I heard someone yelling at him to come quietly, or they'd shoot me. Then I got shot. It gets a little fuzzy after that. I think my father-in-law brought me here."

"So Bayer's behind this?" Holcomb insisted more than he asked.

"What?" Claire's confusion washed away with her realization of who was speaking to her. "Wait a minute, what was your name again?"

"I'm Detective Leon Holcomb, and I'm trying to get to the bottom of what happened to you."

Claire remembered him. It was a while ago, but she remembered the crazed look in his eyes when he asked her about her father-in-law weeks ago. Before she could say anything, a pair of individuals walked into the room, flashing their badges.

"Hey, we're Tawney and Grey with the one-two-two. Who are you?"

"Holcomb, one-nine. Just wrapping up here."

The woman who identified herself as Grey questioned Holcomb immediately, "What's Bay Ridge doing over here across the bridge with no heads up to the cap? You just roaming around our jurisdiction for what?"

The other officer interjected. "And I thought the one-nine was wrapped up in that multi-agency task force?"

"Listen," Holcomb raised his hands in surrender, backing away from Claire. "I'm not here to step on anybody's toes. I was chasing a lead on one of my cases, and it brought me here. I just wanted to see if Mrs. Thompson could be a little more helpful in identifying-"

Detective Grey raised her hand to silence him,

a gesture which grew increasingly annoying to Holcomb. "Can I speak to you outside?"

Holcomb grunted but agreed to leave the room. Once they left, Detective Tawney smiled at Claire and told her, "Mrs. Thompson, please be assured that you are safe here. I want to go over the details of the night in question with you to see if we can catch the people who broke into your home and attacked you and your husband."

So Claire went over the story a few more times with the new detective until Grey returned. She whispered something in her partner's ear before turning to Claire, "We want to apologize for Detective Holcomb's zealous behavior. He shouldn't bother you anymore."

"Is there something wrong?" Claire desperately wanted to know now that flashes of his face were broadsiding her memories.

"No, nothing you need to worry about."

That's all the detective would say about Holcomb, but the words didn't ease Claire in the slightest. Her entire body ignited with anxiety as she truly believed that wouldn't be her last time dealing with Detective Leon Holcomb.

12

Bayer arrived at the same building in Midtown Manhattan that he'd left a few days ago, wondering if Sinclair was going to be inside. He took a chance walking into the lobby of the criminal kingpin's enterprise without an appointment, but he needed to set his plans in motion.

The environment grew plainer with every minute Bayer stood in the lobby. Even with the grey walls surrounding him and stone grey tiles under his feet, there wasn't anything extraordinary outside of the minimalistic security measures. Other than the massive human standing behind the desk, only a few cameras were positioned near the corners of the ceiling. The body scanning technologies were hidden effortlessly in the lines around the lobby.

Bayer continued to look around with uncertainty that he'd have the chance to walk back out. If he had to give anyone details about where he was, the only thing he could say was the address, and even then, the building looked like every other one on the block. This idea seemed a lot smarter the other night when he conjured up this plan.

"Can I help you?" The security guard's voice boomed across the empty lobby, forcing Bayer to approach him.

Bayer started, "Listen, I was here the other day-"

"And?" The guard's expression didn't change.

"I'd like to speak to Mr. Sinclair. I just want to thank him and ask him-"

"Name?"

Bayer grew impatient with the guard's rudeness, but he complied, "Bayer Thompson."

The guard begrudgingly picked up the phone and pushed a button. After mumbling into the receiver, he put the phone down and stared at Bayer. "Stay put. Someone will be down to see you in a minute."

Bayer felt his pulse quicken as he wondered exactly what that meant. He hadn't done anything to deserve the malice of Sinclair. On the other hand, the temperament of criminals wasn't his expertise. Sinclair could find Bayer showing up unannounced as reason enough to kill him.

The ding of the elevator doors opening up drew Bayer's attention to the people stepping off it. He hoped these wouldn't be the last faces he ever saw. The first person was just as big as the security guard standing behind the desk, a mammoth-sized human who could probably toss Bayer around the room even though he wasn't a small man. The second person off the elevator was a woman with long legs, a petite body, and a face that sparked memories from nights long ago, but he couldn't bring them to the forefront of his mind. Her eyes sparkled in the fluorescent lighting and locked onto him with a smirk right before she slid on a pair of shades. The way her hips swayed from side to side like she owned the place made her the focal point of the room. So much so Bayer didn't see Cesar Sinclair walk out a few steps behind her with another pair of armed guards.

Sinclair's voice echoed around the lobby, "You know, Thompson, the only thing my wife likes looking at her that hard is dollars and cents. I'm certain you don't have the dollars, and the way you're watching her, I'm positive you don't have any sense."

Bayer turned to face the man who could end his life with the snap of his fingers and hoped he wasn't truly the jealous type. "You have my apologies, Mr. Sinclair. I just wanted a moment of your time."

Sinclair eyed one of the guards and tipped his head toward his wife, who was already afoot outside the door with her guard holding it open. A single snap of his fingers sent the guard behind the desk around a corner and the one standing between them a few steps away. Once they had the illusion of privacy, Sinclair stood in silence with his hands folded in front of him, "Your moment needs to last less than five minutes, Mr. Thompson."

Bayer nodded, "Of course. I wanted to thank you for the information and location of my son. He and his wife are going to be okay."

"You could have sent that in a postcard. What is it that you want, Mr. Thompson?'

"I need to do some things to protect my family and untie my reputation from yours. To do that, I need a parole officer who's not so invested in what I'm doing every hour of the day."

Sinclair nodded slowly, "So you need a transfer and? A job, perhaps?"

"No!" Bayer rebuffed immediately, "Sorry, but no. I just need the transfer to someone who can give me a bit more freedom. I have a few options for employment lined up."

"I have to admit that I've wanted you on my payroll for quite some time, but Johnie said you'd never go for it. If you change your mind, I want to give you a lot more than an easy transfer to an officer who'll leave you alone."

Bayer shook his head, "No, this is it. Besides, you're not the only person who owes me a thing or two."

"Oh?" Sinclair tipped his head toward the ceiling with amusement riding his face, "I owe you?"

Bayer decided to leave his sarcasm out of the conversation, "Absolutely not; the new PO makes us even."

The two men shook hands, and still, Sinclair admitted, "Somehow, when you say it like that, I feel like I'll never be able to repay you."

Three days passed when Bayer found himself staring into the worried eyes of a woman he knew cared far too much for him. Genevieve stood next to him outside of his new parole officer's building in a surprisingly well-to-do area of Queens. The thick binder she clutched in her hands began to turn her caramel knuckles white.

"I can't believe I'm going along with this," Genevieve hissed.

Bayer patted her on the shoulder, "You're not going along with anything. You're simply fulfilling the request of your parolee to transfer to an office closer to his new residence."

"You don't have a new residence! How are Cory and Claire?" She asked with Bayer, who sensed her eagerness to change the subject.

"They're okay, staying in a hotel until they find a new place to live. Claire refuses to set foot back inside the house, and it's all my fault."

"We both know that's not true, Bayer." Genevieve huffs out a sigh before pulling the binder up to her chest. "I hope you know what you're doing. This guy, he's, well, he's got a reputation for working with many of the people you don't want to be associated with. This is going to look like exactly what you've been avoiding."

"That's my problem. I've been avoiding it instead of facing my problems head-on. I need to embrace and leverage the relationships I have, no matter how fictitious they are."

"But, Detective Holcomb-"

Bayer hushed her with a slight gesture of his hand. "He's going to get exactly what he's expecting."

"He wants you back in prison, and I'm sure that's what he's expecting."

Bayer smirked, "Someone's going to go to prison, and I'm sure it's not going to be me. Are you ready?"

"Ready for what? You haven't told me what you're going to do."

Bayer took her hand into his with a slight squeeze. "I'm going to protect myself, my family, and this damn city from a vendetta no one has any idea being carried out."

With that, Genevieve escorted Bayer into an office building that looked more like a posh business complex than an arm of the parole bureau. She flashed her credentials, and an administrative clerk showed them into a conference room where they waited patiently and quietly. A few minutes later, a man in a costly suit with a very expensive haircut whisked inside of the conference room with a smile so wide it was contagious.

"Good morning Officer Parsons and Mr. Thompson." He shook their hands before they each sat down. "I'm Penny Benziger. I must admit that it is a pleasure to meet The Saint finally."

"The Saint?" Genevieve asked with a raised eyebrow.

"Yes, The Saint. One of the few officers whose parolees don't re-offend and regularly enjoys her job and helping people. I feel like you're in the wrong business."

Bayer stared between the two, conversing like he wasn't even there, and shifted in his seat.

"My apologies," Penny directed at Bayer. "I can get to the point. Officer Parsons needs to leave that binder and any other pertinent information with my secretary, Dana. Bayer and I have a lot to discuss, and I imagine he doesn't want you to be a party to it. As I said, it's a pleasure to meet you, Parsons. It'd be prudent if you left us to talk."

"Give us a moment, please," Bayer told his new PO as he turned to Genevieve.

"I guess I should have just given these to you," she said, motioning toward the binder. "I don't know what I was expecting to happen here."

"You were probably expecting me to fill you in on my plans, but like he said, you're a saint. You're too good at what you do; too good for me to rope you into this and tarnish the reputation you've built. I don't know. Maybe you just wanted to make the introduction, or maybe you thought you'd get to sit in on this meeting?"

Genevieve leaned back in her chair with a stern look in her eyes. "I'm guessing that you already made up your mind that you weren't going to include me. Why'd you let me come here if you knew you weren't going to let that happen?"

"I like you, and I like spending time with you. I don't care if that means spending a half-hour in the car with you taking me to Queens only for us to talk about how bad cabbies drive. I want to thank you for the ride too."

"You're welcome." She pushed herself away from the table. "I'll just head out then. Will I ever see you again?"

"I'd like to think that if you do, our relationship will be on different terms. For now, we need to leave things as they are until this shit with Holcomb blows over." Bayer stood up and thought to hug her, to show her some affection, but with the possibility of it being deemed inappropriate, he remained where he stood. They didn't have anything else to say. The only thing stuck between Genevieve and Bayer was the tension of unrealized passion destined for another day, or perhaps, another life.

13

Penny Benziger held a smirk on his face that made Bayer slightly uneasy. The guy sat there with a head full of slicked-back white hair, a matching white goatee, and blue eyes that beamed with excitement. His entire demeanor was too chipper for Bayer. They sat in his office for a little over an hour while Penny sorted through the binder Genevieve left for him. He appeared to enjoy reading its contents like a comic book.

"She is thorough," Penny chuckled.

"Yeah, so how does this work?" Bayer asked him, wanting to get out of there as soon as possible.

Penny kept the smile on his face as he laid into his new parolee, "Well, I'm a government employee and not an attorney, so understand that what you say to me isn't privileged in the slightest. You're going to show up here whenever I tell you to. You're going to piss in a cup whenever I tell you to. You're going to answer my calls, and you will stick to your curfew and the conditions of your parole, or I will make your life a living hell."

Bayer closed his eyes for a minute, wondering where he'd gone wrong and why this meeting wasn't going the way he thought. After taking a deep breath, Bayer decided to keep his mouth shut.

"What about your residence and place of employment?"

Bayer grimaced. "I am interviewing for apartments this week, and I have decent savings to rely on until I can find suitable employment."

"So not only are you homeless, but you're unemployed. I have to say, Mr. Thompson, you are not the model citizen, and I am worried that you came to my office in hopes of some free ride. You were better off with The Saint. At least she would have helped you get situated. So I have to ask you, what the hell are you doing here?"

"I was referred to you by a friend," Bayer told him as he pulled out the same business card he received the night he took Claire to the hospital. He handed it to the officer whose chipperness faded away the minute he looked at the card. He adjusted the tie around his neck and stood up from his desk. Bayer watched the man head straight for the exit.

Penny looked out of his door, up and down the hallway outside of his office before waving his index finger for Bayer to follow him. They headed toward the elevators and went up to the top floor. Penny refused to say another word as he walked around the corner from the elevators and into the building's staircase. The staircase led to a door that brought them out onto the roof.

Bayer was fed up. "What the hell is going on here?"

"I didn't know you were who you were," Penny said.

Bayer suppressed his irritation for a moment. "What the hell does that mean?"

"That means that I'm a damn good parole officer, and I treat every felon under my supervision the same unless they require special treatment. You coming from The Saint didn't exactly signal to me that you were who you are. I thought you were just trying to get away from the ball buster, or maybe she shot you down or something and transferred you to me on purpose."

"Didn't you get a call about me?"

"No. The way I communicate about matters like this is not over any phone or in any office," he told

Bayer with a wave of his hands in finality. "Shit."

"Listen, Mr. Benziger-"

"Call me Pinch."

Bayer looked at the man for a second, trying to determine if he should continue on this warpath. "Pinch?"

"Yeah, I'm the guy you call," the frazzled officer insisted, rolling his hand in a way to let Bayer finish the statement on his own. "Tell me what you need."

"Okay, Pinch," Bayer shook his head. "I need you to do your job. Everything you said to me in the office will happen. I'll play ball. I just need you to give me a heads up when you're telling me to do all of those things, and I'm going to give you a heads up when I need you to tell me to do all of those things."

Penny, err, Pinch pinched the bridge of his

nose and nodded in agreement with Bayer.
Running his frantic fingers through his white hair
didn't stop his hand from shaking as he spoke, "I
need a fucking cigarette."

"I don't smoke," Bayer shrugged.

"Neither do I," Pinch sighed with his eyes
turned up to the sky. "Okay, so you need an actual
employer and an actual address. Do you have
those lined up already?"

"I can call in a favor for the job and the place I
can get that sooner rather than later. But I think
you should know I have a renegade cop on my
heels."

"How much of a cowboy are we talking about
here?"

Now Bayer's gaze was the one facing the sky.

"The cop got my son hospitalized. I need to get
in front of this before anything fatally permanent

happens. So when he calls you or shows up here, I'm the model fucking citizen you don't think I am."

"Wait a minute. Wait a minute. You have a kid?"

"He's an adult. I also have an ex-wife, a few ex-girlfriends, and a six-year bid hanging over me while I try to put my life back together. All I want to do is put my life together, and I'm going to need your help with that."

"You don't work for Irish."

Bayer eyed the man with concern rippling through his gut. The first time he meets someone under the guise of being associated with Sinclair, and they call him out. He opted for honesty, "I don't. I don't work for either of them but can't tell the cowboy that. I need you to do this for me. You think I magically pulled your name out of a hat or something?"

"The Saint coulda gave it to you."

Bayer cocked his head to the side with a glare telling Pinch he should know better. "The way she was gripping my file, you know more than I do, I'm like a rescue puppy to her. She wants to be the one to save my life."

"How did you get the card?"

"I was given your name in a debt settlement. I don't want to jam you up in any way; I just needed someone with your flexibility. Miss Parsons is inflexible."

Pinch smirked, "Oh yeah? You, uh, know that personally?"

"Pinch, don't get punched."

The officer put his hands up in surrender, "My apologies, I was just curious."

So am I, Bayer thought to himself.

Pinch and Bayer stood on the roof of the building deciding on how flexible their relationship would be. By the time they finished, Bayer had one point of his plan in place with an urgency inside him to get to the others. Now that his family's temporarily safe, he shifted gears and set off to secure employment. He needed someone as flexible as his new PO. While it was a favor, he wasn't ready to cash in; Bayer knew he didn't have any other choice. He'd have to call on someone who cared about him in a way that would open Pandora's box.

A subtle reminder to himself said that Holcomb was to blame for this. Once the rogue detective sent those animals after him and his family, the wrong beast was uncaged. It was high time for Bayer to stop tripping over doing the right thing. He was on the warpath, and the only right thing to do was what was right for him.

14

Bayer sat in a leather chair he knew to be far more expensive than every piece of furniture sitting in the makeshift garage apartment he'd likely never sleep in again. He didn't stand out too much in his denim jeans, vest, and button-up, but still, he looked too comfortable in his clothes amongst the suit-and-ties roaming around the office. He sighed, shifting his weight in the chair and patiently waiting.

The receptionist finally looked up from her screen enough to tell him, "Terribly sorry for the wait, Mr. Tomlin, but please understand that Ms. Rankin is a busy woman who doesn't have time for pop-up visitors. I can schedule you an appointment."

"No," Bayer told her calmly. "It's Thompson, Mr.

Bayer Thompson, and I promise you that if you simply mention my name to her, she'll want to see me."

"May I tell her what this visit pertains to?"

"No."

The receptionist rolled her eyes and went back to work, typing away on her keyboard and still refusing to give Bayer the courtesy he was asking for. The one thing he remained grateful for was she didn't call security on him yet. Or so he thought.

"Sir." A robust and brusk voice addressed him from seemingly out of nowhere. Bayer turned to see a rather large gentleman in a well-fitting shirt and slacks. He folded his beefy arms across his chest to flex, and it didn't faze Bayer in the slightest. "I don't want to make a scene, so I'm going to ask you to come with me to the elevators. I will escort you downstairs and out of this building."

Bayer didn't say anything, but he shot a glare to the receptionist, who did everything in her power to avoid it. He contemplated several scenarios of how this could go, but all of them violated his parole. So he got out of the chair and followed the security guard to the elevator.

"You really should consider making an appointment," the guard told him as they waited for the elevators to arrive.

"I don't need to, and when I come back here and speak to Ava, you'll all see why," Bayer replied, trying to keep his anger from spilling over. Fortunately for him, these people wouldn't have to wait as the elevator doors opened and a woman stood there waiting for the security guard to move out of her way.

Ava Rankin stood at nearly six feet tall with her hair dyed platinum silver and buzzed close to her scalp. The flawlessness of her ebony skin only radiated with the soft brown tone of her eyes. There was a tablet in the crux of her arm, a headset nestled against her ear, and impatience riding her beautiful face. At least, that was until she noticed Bayer.

"Oh my goodness, Bayer! Is that you?!" The CEO of Rankin Consulting & Risk Management beamed at the sight of Bayer standing in front of her. "Come with me! We have to catch up right this instant!"

While Bayer relished in the glow of I told you so, he paused to draw his old friend's attention to a situation. "Ava, before we head into your office, I need you to know that I've been waiting here for nearly an hour. After I'd waited patiently, instead of your receptionist checking with you, she called this guy to escort me out of the building."

"Well, that's not entirely true!" The receptionist shot out of her seat with her face turning red and eyes growing wide.

"Well, if it isn't," Ava scoffed, "Then why is Charles up here? Didn't you check my green list?"

"Um, but, he looked like, and uh-" The receptionist tripped over her words, looking for any excuse to get her out of hot water.

Ava cocked her head to the side, "I want you to see Jenine in HR at the end of business today. Thank you. Charles, please attend to your other duties. Bayer, you come with me."

Bayer eyed some cubicles of people working their hardest for Ava, and he understood why. She was firm but fair. She only asked for you to complete the tasks asked of you. Complete them expertly and she compensated you well for it. It's one of the reasons he hired her so long ago as his Chief Operations Manager. Yet, it seemed like centuries since she was a bright-eyed executive he poached from a competing firm. And now she's running her own business. He couldn't believe how much has changed.

Unlike Cesar Sinclair, Ava could flaunt her success with her penthouse office suites. Her corporation took up the top three floors of an office building in DUMBO. Brooklyn and every single one of her clients were lucky to have her.

As soon as he stepped inside the office, she closed the door behind him and hugged him for a long time. There was a time where she gave him an order, expected him to follow it expertly, and would have compensated him well for his efforts, but he had to turn her down. He didn't want to jeopardize their business with something personal. For a while, she resented him for the rejection, but right now, they were old friends who needed to get reacquainted.

"I can't believe I'm hugging you," she told him while still in his embrace.

"It's okay, I'm fine. I'm here."

She sniffed back a few tears and rushed over to her desk, "Shit, Bayer, you gonna make me ruin my makeup."

"Don't waste any of those tears on me, Ava. I promise you I'm not worth them."

Shaking her head, she stared at him in amazement, "So humble. So fine. And now that I'm thinking about it, so in deep shit! When the hell did you get out?"

Bayer sighed as he plopped down into her chair while she stared out of the large windows overlooking the bustling borough. "About six months ago, but don't be mad at me. I was trying to get myself together without having to come here begging for a handout."

"You know you don't ever have to beg me for shit. I owe you more than I could ever repay you."

Bayer gazed around her office, shaking his head side to side, "No, you did all of this on your own. Seeing you like this is payment enough."

Ava closed her eyes and nodded in agreement. "So what's been going on? You ready to get behind a keyboard again? I can use a Chief Technology Officer."

"Is that even a real position?" he asked with a laugh.

"No, but I'll make it one for you. Full upper management salary and perks, company car, and we'll even get you a loft like the one you had. I'm still mad you sold that place. Whatever you want, name it. It's the least I can do for you leaving me your client book like that. I wouldn't be here today if it weren't for you, and it's about time you cashed in on that favor."

"Oh, don't worry, I'm going to, but differently. I got this renegade detective on my back about this

Sinclair bullshit. He thinks that I'm a goon."

"A goon?!" Ava laughs loudly, a gut-busting laugh that made Bayer wonder if he'd been the nice guy for far too long. "Man, I know you can handle yourself, but a goon?"

"It's not that funny, and what's worse is the set some shit in motion that landed Cory and Claire in the hospital."

"Shit, I'm sorry, Bayer. Are they okay?"

He cleared his throat and sat up in the chair, "They're going to be fine eventually. But the information I have on this guy, I need to make him pay for this shit, and I need to make sure he leaves us alone for good."

"So, what do you need from me?"

"I'm still working out the details, but right now, I need gainful employment worthy of someone who just got out of prison. So no Chief of Nothing. Just get me an entry-level IT tech repair position or something where I can come in every day, clock in, and clock out. I want to give my PO the number to whoever the supervisor is, and for them to say, I'm here, I'm the model employee, and you'd never had a better tech. I need them to say this even when I'm not here."

Ava nodded, "I wish you would have come to me as soon as you got out. I would've been hooked you up. What's the point in knowing people like me if you can't use this relationship to your advantage? I'm going to help you no matter what, but I'm low-key pissed it's like this. Last-minute shit, only when shit hit the fan, you reached out."

"So you want me to take advantage of you?" Bayer laughed.

"You know what I mean. You and that nice guy shit always drove me crazy. What's it got you?"

she asked him.

Bayer sighed, "You're right. I see that more than ever, but honestly, I wanted to pull myself up by myself in my way. I didn't foresee this detective being such a fucking pain. I could have done it, you know? Put my life back together by myself."

"That's bullshit, Bayer, and you fucking know it. Don't give me that pious, holier than thou, spiel. Of course, you could have done it by yourself, but you don't have to, and you won't if I have anything to say about it. People like us who have connections and relationships are supposed to use them. That's the fucking point of networking. You've built an entire network already, and there's plenty of us who don't give a fuck that you did time. We know why you went in, and now that you're out, it's time to get busy. I'll rally the troops for whatever you need, favors you can cash in, anything you can think of."

Friendship is something Bayer hadn't any idea

that he missed so much until this moment. He'd been relying on himself for far too long, and that's what being inside did to him. He wanted to separate himself from Sinclair and Irish so badly that he ended up isolating himself from everyone.

Bayer pulled the file he'd been given in the nondescript brownstone housing his recovering son and tossed it onto Ava's desk. "What's in that stays between us, but I need your help on this."

Ava opened the file, and the first thing she did was lean over Bayer's shoulder to type the link in her computer to pull up the video files Biro showed him a few days ago.

"Oh my god!" She gasped and clutched her

hand over her chest at the sight of Holcomb killing two men in cold blood.

"Those men that were killed, one of them was the son of some crime boss. The detective, Holcomb, made it seem like I did it. Ava, they found my son within hours of this shit. Fucking hours. They shot Claire and beat the crap out of Cory before someone got to them to tell them I had nothing to do with this. I got the file and the footage as part of my pain and suffering compensation." Bayer shook with anger as he relived those treacherous 48 hours all over again through his memories.

"And Holcomb is a cop?! Why don't you take this to the Attorney General? Internal Affairs? The New York Times? Facebook? Somebody? Anybody!" She threw her hands up in frustration.

"Ava, I'm an ex-con who looks eerily similar to the guy in those videos. Have you looked at that file? There aren't any serious blemishes on his record or anything. He's a cop who does his job. No one will take my word over his, especially when there's so much evidence linking me to Sinclair and this Johnie Irish guy. It doesn't help that I got all of this information by way of Sinclair either."

"So what's his problem with you? He almost got Cory killed, and you said Claire got shot? Shit, Bayer, I'm so sorry."

Bayer pinched the bridge of his nose, still in disbelief this was his life. "I don't know what his problem is, but that's what I intend to find out. I don't want you mixed up in this, especially if it comes down to me doin' some shit that may get me locked up again. This nice guy shit ain't get me nowhere, and he almost had my kids killed. I'm already dreading the discussion I have to have with Claire's folks to explain that she landed in the hospital because of me and this bullshit. I need some answers, but I also need some help."

15

Bayer never thought in a million years that he'd have to stoop so low to ask for help. He knew it wasn't stooping, but still, it made him feel like less of a man when he used to be the one helping everyone else.

Ava paced back and forth while Bayer sat at her desk watching the videos of Holcomb killing two men. Flashes of Cory laying in the bed, tubes coming from everywhere, his injuries bandaged; it played over and over again like a broken record. He could barely stomach the images of Claire's barely coherent and limp body running rampant through his memories. It felt like a knife twisting in his chest, turning back and forth, bringing him nothing but agony.

"Okay, I need to make some calls," Ava said to

herself. So she did. A simple push of the button in her headset got someone on the line. "Jenine, I need you up here, now."

"I can go if you need to get back to work," Bayer told her as he began to rise out of her seat.

Ava gently pushed his shoulder down, easing him back into the chair, "Bayer, I need to bring in a few other people on this. Do you trust me?"

"You know I do. I wouldn't be here if I didn't."

"So just relax. You have somewhere else you need to be?" She smirked.

He chuckled, "I'm all yours for now."

"Such a tease," she giggled before returning to her phone calls. "Raye. I'm calling in my chips. Check your messages and meet me for drinks later at that place where that thing happened."

Bayer tuned out the rest of her conversations which ended the minute a short woman knocked on the door and poked her head into the office. She wore pearl white cat-shaped eyeglasses with hints of gold that matched the gold suit she wore. It was the best-looking gold suit Bayer had ever seen. Ava waved the head of her Human Resources Department into the office and offered her the seat in front of her desk.

"Jenine Fletcher, this is Bayer Thompson. I'm going to have his credentials sent to you, but I need this to be discreet. He's going to pilot a position I'm thinking about creating within the IT department. Put him down as an Audit and Network Specialist. Duties include consultations and ongoing customer audits and reports delivered to me, Sales, and Retention. Let's give him full-time entry-level employee benefits. Give Mike a call and have him find a place in"

Ava paused and looked at Bayer, waiting for him to fill in the blanks. He told her. "Queens. I'll even do Long Island City."

Ava returned her attention to Jenine, "Whatever we have from the program should be fine since it's only temporary. When you get a chance, get a new receptionist up here tomorrow morning. Have Ashley moved downstairs to Administration and Clerical. If she doesn't want the position, insist on her resignation. I can't have someone in front of my office, representing me, who can't follow simple instructions."

"Okay, I'll have Ashley taken care of, and once I receive the pertinent details, I'll have the employment package sent to you and Mr. Thompson." Jenine got out of her chair after scribbling a few notes down on a pad.

"Thank you, Mrs. Fletcher." Bayer stood as she did and shook the woman's hand.

After she left, Ava stood there with a smile on her face. "I can't believe you're standing in my office."

"You?" Bayer ran his hand over his face, "I never planned on setting foot in here."

"Don't start that shit again. It's going to piss me off. I know we've been complicated, but I thought we were friends. It hurts me knowing that you didn't want to come and see me."

"You know, asking for help has never been a trait of mine."

Ava rolled her eyes, "Personally, absolutely not. Professionally? Brains superseded your ego all of the time. You hired me, right? You busy tonight?"

Bayer shook his head, "I want to check out the addresses in that file for Holcomb."

"No!" Ava damn near shouted, "Don't do anything stupid. Come out with me tonight, and I promise you won't be disappointed."

"That sounds complicated, and my life is

already complicated enough."

Ava stroked the side of Bayer's face with her delicate fingertips, staring deep into his eyes with adoration and then sadness. She told him, "Bayer, the only thing complicated between us now is why you're assuming I'm trying to make things complicated. I care about you deeply. It used to be a point when I thought I loved you, but that moment has come and gone. You made sure of that. So right now, the only reason why I'm helping you is because I owe you more than the zeroes and commas in my bank account. I owe you more than my name on this company. I'm cashing in a favor from someone who will chew me the fuck out after she reads the message I sent her. I'm using this favor for you. Not only that, you came here as a last resort, and you won't even indulge me in a drink? We're supposed to be friends."

"Ava, I didn't mean-"

She cut him off, "No. Bayer, let me help you.

Raye's going to have some information you can add to that file. I'm sure of it. So I'm going to pretend you're not insulting me by declining the invitation I'm extending to you. I'm going to tell you to leave and see Jenine before you go. She's going to put you in contact with Michael Vincent, who runs our intern program. We take MBAs, set them up here, train them, and then hopefully hire them. We have a few properties around the city where we house anyone from out of state. You'll take one of those properties. Stay there as long as you need."

"That's too much." Bayer's conscience tugged at him. He felt like he was taking advantage of this woman who used to love him, and he'd hate himself for it.

Ava, on the other hand, slapped Bayer upside his head. He hunched his shoulders and shielded his head from any more blows.

"What the fuck?!" He shouted.

Ava laughed and shook her head, "You're an asshole. An arrogant and obnoxious asshole who is forgetting that the reason you're here is that you have some sort of plan to stop this rogue detective from jeopardizing you and your family's safety. Take what's being given to you, Bayer, because I'm almost positive that your stubborn ass is about to get knee-deep in shit. You have a number where I can get a hold of you?"

"Yeah." Bayer pulled out a cell phone, brand new from the one Holcomb smashed and handed it to her. Ava put her phone number in and gave it back to Bayer.

"I'll text you where to meet me tonight. Be dressed to impress. Are you driving?" she asked him.

"No, but please let my pride get me to wherever it is we're going tonight on my own. I can manage a taxi or car. I'm not completely inept or desolate."

16

The address given to Bayer earlier that day brought him to a prestigious hotel. The grandness of the New York City landmark's something rarely seen in newly constructed buildings. Colossal columns, archways, and gold trimmings with a revolving door and yellow lighting to illuminate the night. The red carpet had Bayer stepping over the same spaces as the upper echelon of New York's high society. Although he donned an expensive suit, he wondered how long it would take him to feel normal in it again.

The quietness of the rug under his shoes matched the hushed conversations as he crossed the lobby to the concierge's desk. He felt like an imposter, an outcast with all eyes on him even though a single glance hadn't been cast his way.

However, as soon as the concierge smiled at him, Bayer felt at ease approaching him. He received instructions directing him to the hotel's bar and made his way over, taking notice of the people around him and trying to blend in.

Once he reached the podium out front, he gave his name to the host. Bayer followed the host to a dark booth in the back where Ava sat next to a woman who looked ready to flee the scene of a crime. They were arguing as he approached but stopped as soon as he and the host got within earshot.

The tension between the two women reminded Bayer of the words Ava scalded him within her office. She knew the deed she asked for on his behalf would anger this woman, and still, she did it for him. Bayer sat down, and Ava's other guest looked like she was going to be sick.

"What the fuck, Ava!" The woman hissed. "Is

this who I think it is?"

"Bayer Thompson, this is-" Ava started introductions when the woman beside her cut her off abruptly.

"Let me up from this table right now," the woman snarled. It seemed like Ava knew this would be the woman's reaction as she had her sandwiched between herself and the wall. The woman kept her tone low but still aggressive. "It's never anything easy with you, Ava. But this? This is outright dangerous and stupid. Do you have any idea who this man works for?"

Ava smirked, "Yeah, me."

The woman folded her arms across her chest and slumped deeper into the booth, possibly to remain out of sight while Bayer made his own efforts to keep his face hidden.

"You two are far too paranoid for me," Ava shook her head. "Listen, Raye. Bayer does not work for the people you think he does. As a matter of fact, I need you to tell him what you told me. Please?"

Raye shook her head and kept her voice low, "Fine. There was a murder the same night your incident happened."

"And?" Bayer couldn't care less about other events that took place the night that ruined his life.

"The person killed was a woman named Bianca Alnetti. The details around her murder are closely guarded. It's been leaked around the department that Irish or Sinclair ordered her death."

"Great, another ghost story from my fake boss. So what does that have to do with me?" Bayer asked her.

Raye glanced around like she was ready for someone to come in and snatch her out of her seat. "They connected your story to hers. The guys you were seen talking to that night were deemed to be affiliated with Cesar Sinclair. One of those men killed Alnetti later on that night. The guys you killed were known enemies of Sinclair. That's how everyone knows you work for the syndicate.

The mysterious girl you saw being knocked around, no one can find her. Not on the security footage from that night, nothing. It looks like a plain old hit that pissed so many people off when you plea-bargained your way into a lesser sentence. No one is supposed to do less than ten years for murder."

"It wasn't murder!" Bayer snarled, slamming his fist onto the table. "I took the deal and did my time. I did not push for an early release, but here I am. So I understand why everyone thinks I work for the asshole or why they started thinking I worked for Sinclair. I haven't exactly helped my case either, seeing how I've done several unintentional favors for them."

"I have to go!" Raye said, her voice trembling. "I don't care whether you work for Sinclair or not. I don't want to be seen with you. Ava, we're even. I don't want to hear from you ever again."

"Even Steven," Ava smirked as she stood up to let Raye out of the booth.

Bayer and Ava watched the paranoid woman hustle out of the bar with fear tainting every step. It was only then that Ava signaled the server to come over and take their order.

"Who was that?" Bayer asked once they had some food and drinks on their table.

Ava laughed with a mischievous glare in her eyes that made Bayer uncomfortable. She told him, "That was Raye Bordeaux. About a year ago, there was some charity gala being held here, and let's just say that she should have opted to take her date up to a suite."

"What? You were blackmailing her?" Bayer knew that he shouldn't expect people to be the same, but Ava never struck him as the blackmailing type.

"Of course not," Ave rolled her eyes and palmed something off the table that Bayer didn't realize was there. "She's the aide to someone in a prominent position in the DA's office, and she got caught in a compromising position with someone from the DA's office. She has access to pertinent information that helped you. Well, had."

"What do you want from me, Ava?" Bayer cut to the chase. No one does as much as she's doing for him without strings attached.

Ava slid a thumb drive across the table to him. "That flash drive has every document and piece of evidence associated with your case. It contains detailed conversations your attorney had on your behalf and how they linked you to Cesar Sinclair. It's everything Raye just told us in print. With the information on the drive and the stuff on that detective, there's enough to convince Holcomb that he's locked onto the wrong guy. If it can link you to Sinclair, I'm sure you can use it to unlink yourself."

"How long have you been sitting on this information? And you still haven't told me what you want for doing all of this. Don't give me that we're really good friends bullshit either."

The devious smile spreading across Ava's face suddenly made him remember why he didn't want to cash in any favors from Ava Rankin. There's no way a woman in her position becomes a multimillionaire and CEO of her risk management firm in under ten years without a side of brutality.

"Well, Raye and I were friends at one point. We went out for drinks a few times, and the thing about her is she's entirely too loose-lipped given her previous job. This is only a year or so back, and I don't remember how you came up, but she told me she had access to your files like it was a piece of hot gossip. I asked her to let me see what they had on you, but she refused. Then the gala happened, and so did her indiscretion. She had something I wanted to know, and I had something she didn't want anyone to know. To be honest, I hadn't even thought about it until you came to see me this morning. You're welcome."

"So?" Bayer sighed, waiting for the shoe to drop.

"So, I want you back in the saddle. You are one of the best technology network analysts I know, and it would be a shame to waste your talents. I know you have some things to take care of with that detective, but once it's done, I want you at Rankin. I don't need forever; I just want a few years of your time."

"You really think your clients are going to go for

a convicted felon working and auditing their digital networks and infrastructure?"

"No, but the entry-level salary will keep your name off the billing. No one is going to care who is a member of my consultant team. The worst case is that you don't go in at all. We have a field tech already. He does an okay job, and you can be his eyes and ears back at HQ when it's inappropriate for you to be out in the field with him."

"You've been waiting for me to come to ask you for a job, haven't you?" Bayer tried to keep his anger from bubbling over, but he didn't like being played. He didn't like being manipulated.

Ava shrugged, "Does it matter? You're here now, and it's piss poor business not to take advantage of our relationship, Bayer."

"And if I say no?"

"Bayer, you know the answer to that. Is what I'm asking you so hard to do? I want you to do exactly what you did at TomTech for all those years, just not at the CEO salary level. It's similar work with a fraction of the perks."

"And 75% less pay," he added. "I only need this gig short term, but you want me to hang around for a few years when I could be using that time getting my own company up and running again."

"You know I take good care of my people. I do that because my people are the best. I want you because you're the best. We can talk about letting you explore other employment opportunities after you have a year in."

Bayer shook his head, wishing he'd never come to Ava in the first place. "Can I think about it?"

"Yeah, you have until I finish my drink," Ava smirked before taking a deliberately exaggerated sip from her glass. "Stop acting like working for me is some huge anchor that's dragging you down to the bottom of the Hudson. Don't forget what you're asking me to do either!"

Ava leaned in closer to Bayer, ensuring her voice remained just above a whisper. "You're gonna have me jammed up on fraud charges if your PO looks hard enough on those days you want to be clocked in, but you're not there. And what happens when whatever you're doing about Holcomb comes back to bite me on the ass? I'm taking a risk on you, and I'm in the business, so the rewards had better be damn well worth it! You said it yourself, ain't too many companies you were doing business with gonna be too keen on working with a felon. You thought it was hard before? Wait until you step back into corporate America with a conviction."

Bayer ran his tongue over his teeth, twisting his mouth in frustration because he didn't like being told what to do. He didn't like asking people for shit, and this was one of the reasons why. They always expected something in return.

"Fine. You got me." Bayer conceded.

"Great! I'll make sure you're all set up by the end of the week."

"Thanks," Bayer mumbled. "I'm sorry too, Ava. You're sticking your neck out for me, and the least I can do is put some work in for you. We can review my options at the 18-month mark."

Ava shook her head and chuckled. "I said a year, and that's that. Hopefully, by then, we'll get rid of that annoying ass habit of yours."

"What habit is that?" he asked.

"That nice guy shit. Bayer, it's got to go."

17

Yellow crime scene tape beamed brightly in the afternoon sun, draped across the front door of Cory's home as Bayer walked past the house toward the garage. The sound of Claire's muffled cries haunted him like a whispering spirit, angering him every time he stepped onto the property.

A walkthrough every few days kept squatters from taking up residence, and he agreed to get the house cleaned up and ready for their realtor to show it. The door creaked open when Bayer pushed his way inside the small space he used to call home. He could barely stand it. The pain of the actions set in motion by Holcomb left him reeling in his rage. It suffocated him until he left, forgetting the very reason why he'd stopped by in the first place.

Bayer made his way to the precinct in Bay Ridge, hoping to get a moment with Holcomb and see if he could convince the cop he wasn't one of Sinclair's goons. A hint of fear made him pause outside of the precinct. The idea of another confrontation with Holcomb didn't sit well with him.

"Mornin'," Detective Israel Jessup stood right next to Bayer with a cup of coffee in his hand.

Bayer hardly moved, glancing over at the detective. "Good morning."

"Afternoon actually, and he's not in today," Israel said matter-of-factly.

"Oh."

Israel threw the cup of coffee he'd been sipping on into a trash bin and asked, "You want to go grab a cup of coffee? Lunch?"

Bayer didn't refuse the invitation that seemed more like a demand. Israel walked away from the precinct, with Bayer keeping the same stride until they ended up in an empty fast-food restaurant. It should be busy for the lunch hour, but the place felt more like a ghost town. It made Bayer question if this was going to be some sort of setup. But, how could it be? Israel didn't know he'd show up at the time he did.

The two men sat down, not bothering to order anything, with the detective keeping his fingers laced together on top of the table. Bayer did the same.

"What are you doing out here, Mr. Thompson?" Israel got right to the point.

Bayer let his eyes sweep the empty diner with uneasiness settling around him. "I wanted to get a hold of Detective Holcomb because he has the wrong idea about me."

"Why do you care so much what he thinks about you?"

Bayer wondered how honest to be with Israel, and decided to give him parts of the truth. "He's doing things that affect my family and me. My son is hurt because of him thinking I work for Sinclair's organization."

Israel's face showed he knew nothing about what Bayer said. "What do you mean your son is hurt?"

"He and his wife were hurt because of an incident that your partner kicked off."

"That's a heavy accusation to lay on one of the finest cops I've ever known. You have any proof?"

Bayer huffed and rolled his eyes, "This is why I wanted to speak directly to him."

"Why? So you can back my buddy into a corner? You're a piece of shit for trying to pin some incident on my partner and friend simply because he's the only angry face you can probably retaliate against!"

"I don't bother anybody. I'm just trying to live my life, but I wanted to allow Holcomb to back off because I'm not the man he thinks I am!"

"Did you just threaten my partner?" Israel said with increasing anger.

"No. I just want him to know the truth even if he doesn't want to believe it. The truth is I have nothing to do with Cesar Sinclair or Johnie Irish. I don't work for either of them and never have. The night that connected us is a night I wish I could take back, but I can't. It's pure coincidence that people saw me talking to one of Sinclair's men. I had no idea they'd go off and kill that Bianca woman. I never knew the men I killed were members of his rival organization. I was just defending a woman in trouble when things got out of hand. Right now, I'm just trying to rebuild my life from that night. If I could go back and call you guys instead, I would."

Israel nodded slightly before pushing himself out of his seat, "That's a lot of coincidence for a single night. I'll talk to Holcomb but stay away from him. Don't come near him. Don't contact him. Don't pop up at the precinct like this ever again. He's under enough pressure from this job and doesn't need some ex-con trying to jam him up off a coincidence. You're free to go, for now, Thompson. If you're being honest about just trying to live your life, then keep doing that. If you're trying to get my partner into some shit for revenge, let it go because I'll fuck you up even worse than he ever could."

Bayer tried to keep his expression as stoic as possible, not wanting to add another cop to his list of people who hate him. He could only hope that Israel would pass on the information to make Holcomb back off.

*****

Detective Leon Holcomb sat behind his desk in the 19th precinct with his feet kicked up as he delightfully sipped his blue raspberry slushie. His lunch break was almost over, and he'd been able to find a rhythm again where he liked his job. However, when his partner walked into the office, the tension in the air cut him like a knife. He sat up immediately as the brooding detective closed the door and stood over him with his arms folded across his chest.

"Everything alright, Israel?" Holcomb asked him.

Israel took a deep breath with apparent restraint; his words pushed through gritted teeth, "I know I'm going to sound ridiculous, but I'd rather be wrong than right. Please tell me that your grudge against Thompson has nothing to do with Bianca."

Holcomb's chipper mood faded instantly as he put his feet on the ground and practically lunged out of his chair. "Who the fuck told you that?"

"Oh, shit," Israel's anger faded as his eyes grew wide with frustration, "You've got to be fucking kidding me. That was seven years ago! You're risking your job and your fucking sanity over some broad-"

"I was going to marry her!" Holcomb shouted. "She was my everything!"

"She was a UC, you fucking simp! She wasn't going to marry you. She couldn't! She was fucking one of Sinclair's goons instead of doing her job. She got herself killed! Everything that everyone did to keep that shit quiet, and you're chasing her ghost looking for retribution from a guy who literally has nothing to do with it!" Israel's anger resurfaced with his face burning a bright shade of red.

"Thompson could have placed Sinclair at the club with her killer. He could have linked them! He should have linked them. If he had just done what he was told and placed Sinclair at the club with the triggerman, they could have put Sinclair on the indictment too. It's his fault she's dead!"

"Thompson?"

"NO! SINCLAIR!" Holcomb broke down. "This shit has been eating me up since that night, and I know that Sinclair is the real reason she's dead. I wanted Thompson to buckle and go crying to his boss. That's what they always do. You fuck them up, and they go to their boss."

Israel sighed and pulled a chair over to his partner's desk, "Leon, listen to me and listen to me good. Thompson does not work for Cesar Sinclair or Johnie Irish. Whatever it is that you're doing to him, or his family, to pressure him into running to Sinclair and forcing Sinclair to act ... it's stupid and thoughtless. You need to let this vendetta go.

Please."

"You don't know what you're asking me to do. Bianca was everything to me. You didn't understand our relationship, and Sinclair just yanked her away from me. Thompson is a means to get to Sinclair. He's the weakest link, and I'm going to break him!"

Israel wiped his face with his hands, wishing this conversation never took place, "Bayer Thomspon is a means to an end alright, yours if you're not careful. This obsession with him and Sinclair isn't good for any of us. Work with the task force. Don't just siphon off information from this investigation so you can go in guns blazing and get your man. People lose loved ones every day. That doesn't give any of us an excuse to go out and take justice into our own hands."

Holcomb desperately wanted Israel to back him, telling him, "Sinclair does it every day. Every day, assholes like him get to wave their magic money wands and make their problems disappear. I'm going to put an end to that shit."

"Will you listen to yourself? You're ignoring me completely. I'm telling you that men like Cesar Sinclair don't come down at the hands of a single person. One lone detective doesn't get the job done. All you're going to do is get yourself killed. Thompson was right. You don't care what the truth is."

Holcomb paused for a moment, then tipped his head to the side, "What do you mean Thompson was right? When did you speak with him?"

"Today," Israel sighed, "He came by and wanted to speak with you, but I'm sure that would have ended in catastrophe, especially after the last time he showed up. I sent him away. He won't be bothering you, and you need to leave him alone!"

18

Holcomb moved like a man on a mission. He left his precinct without explanation, fueled by determination to get to Bayer Thompson.

"How dare he?!" Holcomb muttered to himself. It's all he could think about as he hopped in a squad car to take the trip out to Thompson's last known address in Staten Island. He dreaded being in the borough, very much so like most of its residents.

By the time he reached the home on Maple Drive, the crime scene tape had obstructed his path like an instant roadblock. Holcomb tore it away from the door and walked inside. It was practically empty. There weren't any pictures on the walls or any furniture in the rooms. He moved down the hall toward the kitchen, which was immaculately clean. Signs of a crime happening were scrubbed away some time ago. After pulling a pen out of his pocket, Holcomb used it to open the cabinets and drawers to find it all empty. He went through the entire house to see no one has lived here for a while.

Blood surged through his body, coursing with his adrenaline, as Holcomb thought the most ludicrous ideas. They probably skipped town! It took a matter of seconds for Holcomb to get on the phone, dialing numbers furiously. He needed to know where the Thompson family went.

The first call he made was to the detectives covering the home invasion that he incited. Granted, Holcomb wasn't in the clearest state of mind, but he did his best not to let his anger come through once the detectives answered the phone. They weren't as forthcoming with the information as he would have liked, but he got an answer.

The Thompsons never came back to the home

after they recuperated from their injuries. They were staying in a posh apartment somewhere in Queens. That irritated him even further because he'd have to stomach evening rush hour through the boroughs just to get there. His next call was to Thompson's parole officer. The office gave him the run around to the point where he decided to show up there himself.

Once Holcomb was standing in front of Genevieve Parsons, he tried to remain professional, but her beauty was undoubtedly a calming distraction. However, the glare in her eyes told him she wouldn't entertain flattery of any kind from him.

"I need to speak with Bayer Thompson." He demanded of Genevieve.

She didn't care. "I can't help you."

"That can't be true. I was told that you go above and beyond to be helpful. Now, please get your parolee down here," Holcomb sneered.

She shrugged, "I go above and beyond often, and if Bayer Thompson were still under my purview, you'd have my full support. However, Bayer moved and changed POs, so talk to Officer Penny Benziger. I'm sure you can find the office's information on your own. Now, if you don't mind, I need to get back to work."

"Why isn't the system updated? You're still listed as his point of contact."

Genevieve continued to sit behind her desk, unmoved by the moody detective. "I've done everything I'm supposed to do on my end. It's not up to me to make sure the city's database reflects new changes. When it updates, it updates. Now, if there's some sort of emergency, then call the police."

"Are you in a relationship with Bayer Thompson?" Holcomb blurted out. His heart raced as he fished for information. He wanted Bayer to hurt the same way he did. He wanted Sinclair to hurt the same way he did. It was getting to the point where Holcomb didn't care who paid for the death of his girlfriend. Someone needs to face justice for her death. While he preferred Sinclair, he rationalized that bringing down Bayer Thompson would get him that much closer to the man playing the nemesis in his life. Justice would prevail by any means necessary.

"Wow, so because I'm not bending over backward to get you the information you want, I have to be sleeping with him? The answer to that is no; I'm not." She snapped. "And, even if I was, that's none of your business. He's no longer in my caseload. If there's nothing else you need, Detective, I need to get back to work."

Holcomb would have stood in front of Genevieve's desk to argue her down. Still, despite current circumstances, they were on the same side, trying to keep society safe from people like Bayer Thompson and his known, or unknown, associates. So he left her office, hopped in his squad car, and began the battle against evening rush hour to head toward the only other address he might get some help.

Traveling from Brooklyn to Queens should only take 10 to 15 minutes, but it reached the 90-minute mark easily during rush hour. Holcomb took the ride in silence, tuning out the mindless droning of the radio, the blaring horns of trucks and cars fighting for space on the BQE, and dodged potholes.

By the time he made it to the newest Thompson address, he was more frustrated than when he left Israel at the precinct. He couldn't believe his partner didn't understand how vital bringing Thompson and Sinclair to justice was. It didn't matter that Thompson could explain his connection as coincidence. A cop died, and the city acted like nothing happened. Holcomb felt like he was the only cop left in the world who cared about Bianca Alnetti.

The three loud pounds of Holcomb's fist against the Thompsons' front door rattled the frame. He heard some rustling from inside before the mumbling voices reached him. Suddenly, one boomed from behind the door, "Who is it?"

"NYPD! It's Detective Holcomb! Can I have a word with Bayer Thompson, please?"

After further muffled conversations, the door finally opened for Holcomb to see Cory Thompson standing there shirtless. His ribs were bandaged, and his arm was in a sling. There were remnants of bruises and scratches across his chest, and a black eye was fading. Holcomb stared into the face of the young man as a pang of guilt washed over him and drowned out some of his rage.

"My Pops is at work. He doesn't live here, but I

can give him a message." Cory said without any emotion in his voice.

Holcomb shifted uncomfortably, "Listen. Tell him that coming to my job, to my precinct, is a recipe for disaster. It's going to get him, and his boss tagged for metal bracelets. You feel me?"

"No," Cory sighed. "I don't know what you're talking about, but my Dad's been at work all day. You can check with his job and his PO."

"So you're calling my partner a liar?" Holcomb questioned.

"I don't know your partner. I don't know you. You can talk to his PO-"

Holcomb cut him off, "I'm done with you all giving me the run around about this piece of shit of a human being!"

"Who the fuck are you calling a piece of shit?!" Cory's anger surfaced, but his wife appeared behind him with a soft hand to his shoulder. She eyed Holcomb and whispered in Cory's ear before she limped away. He took a deep breath before addressing the detective again, "You have my apologies. I don't know the whereabouts of Bayer Thompson. If you have any questions, please take them to his parole officer, Penny Benziger. Have a good day."

Cory went to close the door but was stopped by Holcomb's foot.

"Please remove your foot from inside of my home, Detective." Cory squared his stance, readying himself to stop the officer from forcing his way in, and called out to his wife, "Babe. Call Detective Grey and Tawney, please. Then call the local police. After that, call Mr. Sanchez and then New York 1."

Holcomb moved his foot but used his forearm to keep the door open. "You don't have any idea the kind of man you're protecting. By protecting

Bayer Thompson, you're helping to shield men like Cesar Sinclair from the justice coming for them."

"I'm not a cop. It's not my job to bring anyone to justice. If you can't do your job without harassing innocent people, you need to get a new one. I will die on this doorstep before I let you set foot in here and harm my wife. You've upset her more than enough, and if you do it again, we're going to have problems. You feel me?"

"Are you … Are you threatening a New York City police officer?" Holcomb eyed Cory with a crazed expression riding his face.

"Absolutely not," Cory stated. "I'm simply telling you facts. Now, please. My wife and I are about to sit down to dinner. Leave us alone. For any information regarding my father, you can speak to his PO, Benziger. You can also reach out to his attorney, Martin Sanchez. Or if you're really in desperate need and he wants to make himself available to you, you can call him yourself. Have a good day, Detective."

With that, Cory closed the door, and Holcomb let it shut. Every intention of throwing Bayer in cuffs when he saw him flew out the window. So, he gave up his search for the night and decided to go home, allowing himself time to come up with more robust tactics. If inciting a war between underworld factions didn't turn out the way it was supposed to, he'd have to try something different. He needed to find another way to break Bayer Thomspon and force him to go to Sinclair for help. It had to help to expose the syndicate and its leader for the menacing plagues on society they truly were.

It's all Holcomb could think about as they mumbled the words to himself, "The gloves come off now. No more Mr. Nice Guy."

19

Holcomb walked into his office to see Sergeant Adam Vega talking to Israel by his desk. A groan escaped his lips. The only reason Adam would be in his office this early before his shift even started was to give him a headache over some bullshit.

"Holcomb, just the cop I wanted to see. You are still a cop, right?" Adam asked with a chuckle.

A pit of uneasiness rolled through Holcomb's stomach. Could his sergeant have any ideas about what he'd been up to? Slow and deliberate breaths kept his heart from beating out of his chest. It didn't silence his pulse from beating like a bass drum against the inside of his head.

"Morning, Sarge. What's going on?" Holcomb asked with a glance at Israel. Israel shrugged, giving him no hint at what was coming.

"You two were moved off of cold cases to help with this multi-agency task force. I hear great things about Israel here, but Leon, you seem to get left out of the conversation pretty often. So I go to myself, 'Why is that?'"

"I don't know, Sir," Holcomb replied.

"That was rhetorical, asshole." Adam continued, "Then at seven in the morning, I'm getting calls. Is it about Detective Leon Holcomb? Yes, it is. Is it good things like I hear about Israel? No, no, it is not. I am getting complaints from a woman who was shot in the goddamn leg by home invaders, the cops working her case all the way across the Verrazzano, the woman's husband who's recovering from several broken bones which he sustained trying to protect his wife during said home invasion, and the Chief of Dees also breathing down my neck about some cowboy vigilante bullshit. I say that's not my cop. That's not my detective working Cesar Sinclair like that because we're a part of a motherfucking task force. So tell me, Holcomb, why am I getting complaints?"

Holcomb tried to explain himself, "I found an angle, and I needed to see it through. Bayer Thompson-"

Adam cut him off, "Bayer Thompson is not a player in this game. He is as much connected to Cesar Sinclair as I'm connected to motherfucking Santa Claus. Every link between them is purely circumstantial at best. If you have something concrete, please, tell me now. I'll walk out of here and leave you alone to do your job. I'll even apologize for wasting your time and my breath. What do you got?"

"The DA's case had Thompson talking to the trigger man for Bianca, and Thomspon could have linked him to Sinclair from the club that night. I've been surveilling Thompson to see if he leads me to Sinclair, Irish, or the trigger man."

"Let me guess, you got nothing, right?" Adam sneered.

"Well-"

"Before you lie to me, Detective, speak to me like I already know the answer."

"I'm still waiting for Thompson to reach out to Sinclair or any of his people. I know he will."

"NO! No, he won't. But do you know who he has reached out to?" Adam's eyes grew wide, but Holcomb shook his head side to side since he didn't know. The sergeant sighed, "Ava Fucking Rankin. I'm gonna guess that you have no idea who that is. You wouldn't because she's a civilian. Ava Rankin is a consultant under contract with several businesses including local government agencies. I say that to say this. She's a big fucking deal, and Thompson hired her before he went in.

Guess who he works for now that he's out?"

"Ava Rankin?" Holcomb mumbled.

"Bingo, hotshot! I don't know whose buttons you've been pushing these past few weeks, but cut it the fuck out. I don't want seven a.m. phone calls. It's bad for my ulcer. Work the assignments given to you like good little boys and do your fucking jobs. Your little passion project with Bayer Thompson is over. Bianca Alnetti, God rest her soul, is dead. Let it go. Everybody went to jail that night. What the fuck are you so pissed about?"

"Everybody but Sinclair!" Holcomb blurted out.

"Well, guess what the fucking task force is for? Genius. Do your damn job Leon, or I'll get a rookie to come in here and do it for you."

The sergeant left the office, leaving Holcomb to stew over his reprimand. He couldn't believe that Israel didn't say anything to defend him. He eyed his partner like he'd been betrayed. "You should've said something."

Israel smirked as he sipped his coffee, "I did say something, several times as I remember. I told you to leave Thompson alone. No one gives a fuck what Bayer Thompson is up to on any scale of this investigation. It's like we're all going duck hunting, but you want to go skiing."

"What?" Holcomb raised an eyebrow.

"Exactly," Israel pointed at him, "They have nothing to do with the other. Today's assignment is bodyguard surveillance. We're supposed to tail this guy Charles Tennison for the next few days and see what pops up. He may or may not be a new goon for Sinclair or Irish."

"Fine," Holcomb huffed. "Where do we start?"

Israel tossed a folder to him, "His place of residence."

The detectives got themselves ready for the day and headed out into the New York City morning rush with Holcomb upset at his loss of freedom to pursue the one suspect he had in mind. They found themselves outside of an apartment building in the Lower East Side of Manhattan. After ensuring their target was indeed home, they did what they were assigned to do; they waited and watched.

Surveillance of a random man named Charles Tenison lasted three days, with Holcomb and Israel following him through his daily routine. His day consisted of two trips to the gym, a visit to the local health food store, and a stop at a vitamin and supplement shop. They watched him go to the post office and get his car cleaned. It was the life of someone who appeared to obey the law, and Holcomb was getting antsy. On the fourth day of their surveillance, they followed their target to a building in Downtown Brooklyn. The detectives made sure to add the address to their notes, and even more so, they noticed who approached the building alongside Charles Tenison.

Holcomb smashed his fist against the steering wheel and growled, "Un-fucking-believable."

Israel pushed himself upright in the front passenger seat of the car they'd been practically living in for the past few days to see Bayer Thompson walking up to their subject. It didn't take long for Holcomb to get himself together, checking to make sure he had his gun and badge on him as he started to get out of the car.

"Where do you think you're going?" Israel asked with a firm grip on Holcomb's forearm.

"I'm going to get a closer look. Stay here in case one of them runs."

"Leon, please," Israel pleaded, "Whatever it is you're thinking about doing, don't. You can jeopardize this entire investigation."

Instead of heeding his partner's cautionary words, Holcomb shook his arm from Israel's grasp, got out of the car, and scurried across the street. It wasn't too hard to remain inconspicuous as he blended into the hustle and bustle of commuters traveling up and down the sidewalk. He hung back, watching the two men sip their coffee before passing through the building's main entrance. A glance at his watch told Holcomb it was barely past eight, and he wanted to know what these known affiliates of Cesar Sinclair were up to.

The thrumming of his heart beating loudly in his ears drowned out the sound of the morning traffic. Every breath, every step, it all synced as he moved closer to the entrance without a plan in mind. Once he reached the double-door entryway, he peeked inside to see their target. Charles was a monstrous human being. Watching him from afar didn't do the man's size any justice at all. He had to be over six feet and well over 250 pounds, probably nearing the 300-mark of pure muscle.

Holcomb watched Charles go behind the reception desk and bend down to retrieve something while trying to keep Bayer in his sights as well. The two men were so deep in their conversation; they didn't notice the detective's face peeking in and out from behind the wall next to the entrance. Charles brought up a large metal case where he put in a combination code to unlock it. He removed some of the items, including a smaller box that looked a lot like a gun safe.

Holcomb continued to surveil them when Charles stripped his belt off and replaced it with a utility belt equipped with a holster. The mammoth-sized security guard opened the gun safe. The detective's anger and frustration for every day Sinclair breathed a molecule of free air led up to this moment of pure adrenaline. He didn't think to watch the two any further. He'd violate Bayer and send him running to Sinclair for help. It could work. It had to.

At the very moment Holcomb reached the door handle to head inside of the building, he heard his name being called. Israel remained across the street with his hands cupped around his mouth, shouting something inaudible. The hand reaching out to Holcomb triggered a knee-jerk reaction from the detective. It was instinct. He hadn't heard the voice of his partner or the voice of the woman walking up behind him. The only sound Holcomb heard was that of his fist connecting to the woman's face and her scream of agony as she hit the wall and slid down to the pavement.

20

"For the last time, it was self-defense," Holcomb snarled as he sat in his sergeant's office, facing his lieutenant, captain, and chief while they ripped him a new one.

"You know what has to happen here, right?" The Chief of Detectives questioned, eyeing the other men. "Make this, and him, disappear. I don't care if he's gotta shovel horse shit on parade duty in Yonkers when he comes back. Ava Rankin has filed a restraining order against you, and I'm sure a civil suit is on its way. Let's not even mention if she decides to really throw her weight around and disrupt business. I don't have all day for this bullshit. I trust you can all handle what comes next. You have my signature and approval on whatever disciplinary action is to be taken. Let's hope they stop running the clip on the news in a few days."

The Chief of Detectives and captain left the office after signing off on a few documents, leaving Holcomb alone with Lieutenant Harbor and Sergeant Vega.

"I told you already. She shouldn't have come up behind me like that. That's a natural reaction!" Holcomb continued to defend his actions. "Who walks up on a cop like that? And, what did he mean by, 'when I come back? Where am I going?"

"On administrative leave," his lieutenant answered. "Effective immediately, without pay pending further investigation."

"You can't do this!" Holcomb shouted. "I was just doing my damn job! Why is this fucking happening? You're all acting like you're trying to protect Sinclair!"

"No one is protecting that asshole, but you're

sure making it harder for us to bring a case against him with you blundering around the city like a bull in a china shop. The real question is, why the hell did you get out of your car in the first place!" The lieutenant shouted.

His sergeant, Adam, jumped in. "Your assignment was clear. None of that said to run personal interference with the target of your surveillance. You had no probable cause to get out of your car."

Holcomb took a deep breath and tried to make his actions make sense, "I saw Charles Tenison, our target, handling a weapon, and accompanied by Bayer Thompson, a known affiliate of Cesar Sinclair, who's on parole. I was going to move in and intercept a possible handoff to violate Thompson and get him to reach out to Sinclair. Sinclair would move mountains to help this guy, and none of us know why."

The lieutenant leaned against the wall while

Adam sat behind his desk. They stared at each other briefly before Adam spoke in a low tone, "And we'll never get the answer to that because of you. The Thompson family filed a restraining order against you as well. Have you been harassing a family that survived a home invasion? The one-two-two had some pretty interesting things to say about you stomping all over their jurisdiction in Staten Island. I also got a call from the local out of Long Island City. What the fuck are you doing out here, Holcomb? You're not just trashing your reputation and tanking your career; you're sullying the good name of the one nine in the process."

Lieutenant Harbor jumped in, "We all want the same thing, but you're behaving like we don't. Do you think Bianca is the only cop to lose their life at the hands of Cesar Sinclair or Johnie Irish? Your emotional rampage has done irreparable damage to this investigation and to the relationships we've been cultivating with all of these other agencies. You know how hard it is to get the IRS, FBI, DEA,

ATF, and NYPD to all work together cohesively?
Do you understand how large an organization
Sinclair and Irish are running, and you think you
can bring them down on your own by fucking with
the lowest man on the totem pole? Hell,
Thompson isn't even an affiliate if I'm reading the
case notes right. All of his links to Sinclair are
circumstantial. The lowest man on the pole isn't
even on it! You jeopardized months of work due to
a personal vendetta. I need your badge and your
service weapon. Get some help, Holcomb. You're
dismissed."

The lieutenant's words lingered in the air like a
tune Holcomb heard before but couldn't remember
the words too. He never thought it would be him.
He was doing the right thing!

The hours of the day passed in the blink of an
eye for Holcomb until he found himself in a dive
bar somewhere in the bowels of Brooklyn.
Napkins, crumbs of food, old pieces of chewing

gum littered the floor, trampled over until they blended into the tiles. The barstools were ripped, stuffing peeked out like wispy strands of hair fraying many of the cushions. Some of the stools were dented after surviving a brawl or two. Scents of smoke, booze, and pity wafted through the air, with its stench clinging to anyone sitting inside for more than a few minutes.

Holcomb had been there over an hour, drowning his sorrows with glass after glass of cognac. He'd invited Israel to come out and drink with him, but his partner declined. He should have expected it. Becoming the department leper made finding a drinking buddy nearly impossible.

"How ya doin tonight, Sugah?" A sultry voice asked from behind him.

Holcomb, heavily intoxicated, turned to face the vixen, "Don't come up behind me like that! You could get punched in the face."

"Honey, the way you're slurring and swaying, you couldn't punch the air," she laughed. "You want some company tonight?"

"Oh," Holcomb's eyes grew wide as he assumed the woman talking to him was a working girl. "I'd love company tonight, but I'm broke. And you may not like me. I'm a cop."

Holcomb drunkenly fished for his badge when it dawned on him he no longer had it. He pouted as he slammed his head onto his arms, folded on top of the bar, "Aw, man. See? They took it from me."

"You seem like a good time to me. I'm sure we can work something out. My name's Peaches."

Holcomb's drunken gaze etched every inch of Peaches' body into his mind. She wasn't the prettiest thing in the world. The life she lived was well worn on her face and in her clothes. Every decision she ever made had left its mark on her, from the bags under her eyes to wrinkles around her mouth. Her pale alabaster skin was in desperate need of sunlight, food, and soap, but there was something about her that made her easy to talk to.

"Take a walk, Peaches," Israel's voice sliced through Holcomb's mind, disrupting his illusions of Peaches' beauty. He sat down next to the disgraced detective and ordered a cranberry juice. Dried water spots and fingerprints all over the glass made it a forensic expert's wet dream, but the idea of putting his mouth on it instantly churned his stomach. Israel left the glass exactly where it was and decided to try and help Holcomb again, "Why don't you let me take you home, Leon?"

Holcomb shook his head from side to side, "Nope! I'm going to take Peaches home."

Israel turned his face up as he looked over his shoulder at the woman. Peaches held the body of someone long out of their prime, desperately trying to hang onto it. Her limbs were skinny with skin that looked far too soft. She sagged in places he never thought a woman could, and her energy screamed of bad decisions. Stringy and dirty blonde-dyed hair with heavily applied makeup didn't better the sight before him in any way. He needed to get Holcomb out of there, even if it would be the last favor he could do for his partner. His glare found Peaches again, staring at him.

"Don't knock it til you try it!" She shouted while gyrating her hips that made him nearly gag.

He shook his head, turning his attention back to the drunk detective on the brink of ruining his life. "There's a rumor going around that IAB's got a file on you too. I really hope what they're saying isn't true. With everything going on, Leon, the last thing you need is to be busted with a pro. Come on, let me take you home."

"NO!" Holcomb pushed himself off the barstool

and away from his partner. "Peaches! Let's get out of here and make some cobbler."

Israel frowned at the innuendo and watched his partner leave the bar with the woman. He should arrest her, but he was off duty, and technically she hadn't solicited any services. If he had to be honest, he assumed she was a hooker, but there wasn't any actual evidence of the sort. So he left his cranberry juice on the counter untouched, paid his bill, and chased his partner out of the bar only to find they were gone.

Holcomb had wandered off into the night without a voice of reason beside him, and there wasn't anything Israel could do about it. He went home and left Holcomb to continue making piss poor life choices.

*****

The intense pounding in Holcomb's head when he woke up the following day made his eyes hurt.

His mouth was as dry as the Sahara, and he had to take a piss like he'd been holding it in for days. The minute Holcomb got out of bed, the room around him spun like a top and put him on his ass. He had to drag his body, arm over arm, to the bathroom of what looked like a rundown studio apartment. Every time he tried to straighten his head, it made him nauseous, and sit back down on the cold floor.

Hours or minutes passed with Holcomb sitting on the bathroom floor before he remembered he had to pee. It took every ounce of strength to pull himself up to the sink and stare the faucet in the eye. The mist of the water gushing from it gave him hope as he splashed some on his face. Finally able to stand upright without tipping over, he steadied himself to avoid swaying and luring the nausea wrestling with his stomach back to the top of his throat. A quick peek out of the door showed the lump of a body in the bed. Regret surged through him like an anxiety attack.

His only grateful moment was seeing used condoms and wrappers all over the room. Hopes and wishes poured out of him silently that he used them all night.

"Hey!" his voice came out rougher than he wanted. After clearing his throat, he tried again, "Hey! You! Get up! Where are we?"

There weren't any windows that he could see out of, but he knew they had to be somewhere near the bar. Maybe in an apartment above it?

Holcomb shook the lump until the sheet uncovered her face. It looked frozen in time, sleeping beauty after one too many martinis and a hard life getting banged in the castle. He shook the woman again with a little more force, and still, she didn't move. She didn't make a sound. He held his finger under her nose and couldn't feel a breath.

Panic replaced his regret and anxiety as his eyes scanned the chaos around him. Clothes were strewn about. Condoms. Drugs. Liquor. It read like a bad scene out of a film. He desperately searched for his pants and finally found them under the beat-up sofa in the dingy studio apartment. Thankfully his phone was still on, and it was filled with text messages and missed calls, but Israel was the only person he called back.

"I need your help!" Holcomb shouted once Israel picked up the phone. "I think she's dead. You need to come help me."

"What the fuck, Leon! I'm on my way."

21

When Israel finally arrived, Holcomb was pacing the apartment, only wearing his jeans and biting his nails. It was Israel's knock and voice from the other side of the door that brought him back to reality.

"Leon, open up!"

The door opened, and Israel stepped inside. The detective looked around before heading directly over to the woman on the bed. It only took him a minute to assess the situation before he started asking questions.

"Leon, focus. What did she take last night?" Israel asked.

"I don't know. I was fucking tossed. How did

you get here so fast? How did you find me?"

Israel rolled his eyes with a nod to the phone in Holcomb's hand. "Your location is on. I should have looked it up last night and dragged your ass home. This is the last place I expected to find you, man."

Israel sighed with disgust and judgment at the sight of condom wrappers. He shook his head, trying to rid his imagination of the torrid night these two may have shared. He looked to Holcomb for answers, but the detective had resumed his pacing and was now mumbling to himself. So Israel checked the woman's pulse and grew angry, "Why haven't you called an ambulance? She's still breathing, you dickhead! She probably o-deed. I need to know what she took! Leon!"

Holcomb shrugged and pointed to a general area near the nightstand next to the bed while Israel got his phone out and dialed, "This is Detective Israel Jessup, badge number 22029; I need a bus at-"

Before he could finish rattling off the necessary details, he was jumped by Holcomb. "You can't! Don't call them! We need to get rid of her body. We need to get out of here! You said it yourself, IAB is after me! They can't find me like this! No one can! I called you because I needed your help!"

Israel pushed Holcomb off of him and looked around for his phone, "You fuckin psychopath! You're right. You do need help! Calm the fuck down! We need to get her to the hospital and you a cup of coffee to sober the fuck up."

Israel spotted his phone, picked it up to his ear, and thankfully the operator was still on the line. He went to speak but again was broadsided by the spiraling detective. It became evident to Holcomb at that moment that he needed to subdue Israel before he ruined his already tarnished life.

Holcomb landed two punches to the jaw before

Israel was able to flip him over and land a few blows to his ribs which knocked the wind out of Holcomb. Wheezing and curled in a fetal position, Holcomb held his hand out to stop Israel from hitting him anymore. It worked as Israel wiped the blood off his lip and stood up. He grabbed Holcomb by the hand and helped him up to his feet.

"I know this shit seems crazy and that you're going to get buried under it, but we need to do the right thing here," Israel told him. "We need to get her to the hospital, and at the very least, we need to get you into your own bed. Just let me help you."

Holcomb nodded, but his sanity and logic didn't last long. He grabbed Israel by the shoulders and shoved him back. "You don't get it! You never did! We never get shit done doing the right thing!"

Israel lost his balance, stumbling backward over Holcomb's boot, and fell. His head hit the corner of the nightstand with a sickening crack. His shoulders and everything beneath them twisted in the opposite direction of his neck before hitting the floor. Convulsions came within seconds, shaking Israel's awkwardly angled body. The sight horrified Holcomb to the point where he didn't know what to do. Time froze around him, and he wished he could go back and keep driving down that road instead of stopping Bayer Thompson on that cold October morning.

In an instant, his panic cleared away, and he went into survival mode. He'd get the blame for all of this. They'd make him the scapegoat. They'd probably blame their failed investigation into Sinclair on him too. So Holcomb begrudgingly fished his boot out from under Israel's trembling body, crawled on his belly to grab the other one that slid under the bed, and frantically sought out his shirt. He tried to remember if he had anything else when he came last night, but that was a fool's errand. He made up his mind that once he was far enough from the scene, he'd call in help for Israel.

The former detective hauled ass out of the grungy studio apartment. He looked up and down the hallway until he saw the window at the end of the hall with the brightness of the morning shining like a beacon of hope, illuminating the way to his new life. There was a fire escape outside of it. He ran over to it with the laces of his untied boots moving in the wind with every stride. Holcomb tried his best to open the window only to find it sealed shut. A movement to the right of him drew his attention to the staircase. Someone had just walked by, and he poked his head inside to see if there was anyone else in there.

He looked up to see he was a few floors from the top and about two floors up from the street. Holcomb took the steps two at a time, twisting his ankle on the way in his loosely worn boots. By the time he hobbled into the sunlight of the spring morning, the only thing he could see was an army of squad cars pulling up to the scene of his crimes.

The woman from last night had taken him to an apartment above the bar, as he thought. His friend, his partner, Detective Israel Jessup, lay in that apartment dying on the floor next to a woman who would pass away before she ever reached the hospital.

Holcomb felt the rough concrete against the side of his face as he was knocked down and placed under arrest. Memories of him slamming Bayer Thompson against the side of a building months ago mirrored his demise.

Israel's call never disconnected. The operator dispatched units to their location immediately. While they didn't know Holcomb was a part of anything at first, his disheveled and frantic appearance was enough for the officers on scene to detain him. His life was over, ruined, and all he ever wanted to do was the right thing.

22

Bayer watched Detective Holcomb from across the street as the vigilante cop glanced over his shoulder before entering the home. He'd been following Holcomb for a few weeks now. The trial for those two bodies in a shoddy apartment he got caught running out of had yet to be set, and it annoyed Bayer that this man got to come home and wait. Bayer didn't care about bail or him being a former police officer. All Bayer knew was that justice rang differently for different people.

It wasn't the first time Bayer watched Holcomb at his place of residence. He'd actually been there several times already. Today was a long day as he tracked Holcomb's weekly meetings at the District Attorney's office, One Police Plaza, the union rep, and his attorney. Curiosity made him wonder what was discussed in those meetings, but Bayer's plan only served one purpose.

He clung to the shadows, watching as cops drove up and down the block. Their timing was too routine. Anyone could break into Holcomb's home, and no one would be the wiser, but who would do something like that?

Bayer grinned to himself as he made his way across the street, knowing he'd have two hours before the cops came back around.

There were some news reports about this incident sparking a rift through the city. Some wanted to allow Holcomb to use his grief as a weapon. Others wanted him to pay for the lives lost due to his reckless behavior. Bayer only wanted him to pay for the torment brought upon his family.

The night was quiet as Bayer broke into Holcomb's house. It was easy enough deactivating his home alarm system as the ex-detective recently bought it through one of Ava's clients. He shook away images of Ava's manipulative smile from his head, not wanting her to disrupt his plans in any way.

Silence filled the two-story home after he came in through a sliding patio door in the backyard. The homes on each side of the house were dark, and he was certain they wouldn't pay attention to a cop-killing asshole in the middle of the night. Bayer flexed his gloved hand in and out, making a fist, ensuring the durability of the leather gloves would last.

He passed through the first floor, moving across the den and making his way into the hallway. Darkness engulfed him mostly, except for the kitchen where Bayer saw an opened bottle of Bourbon on the counter next to an empty glass and a bottle of pills. He looked at the label to see they were mild pain killers, but that was enough for him. He'd followed Holcomb over the past few weeks so often he had his nightly routine down to the minute.

The sound of the shower running upstairs let Bayer know he was right on schedule. Bayer eyed the stairs for a moment, contemplating if his plan of attack was the best, but he couldn't turn back now. His heartbeat thumped inside of his ears with adrenaline rushing through this body.

The staircase was alongside the right wall of the home, leading directly to the front door, which Bayer unlocked. The iron spindles running up to the second floor kept the banister sturdy as Bayer used every muscle in his body to spring up and grab two of them. He pulled himself up and over to bypass the steps he knew creaked loud enough to let anyone in the house know someone was inside and making their way up.

The shower shut off just as Bayer reached the second floor. He peeked inside of the bedroom to see Holcomb with a towel wrapped around his waist and sip the last of what looked like another glass of Bourbon.

"Mm, that's damn good," Holcomb muttered to himself, still with his back to the entrance of the bedroom.

Bayer was thankful for the lack of mirrors as he watched Holcomb turn on the television and fall back onto the bed, letting the late-night movie lullaby him to sleep. It didn't take long as sounds of snoring echoed around the room, louder than the TV with Holcomb turning around to lay on his stomach. Bayer moved in quietly and pulled out a knife. He kept the blade folded in and tucked inside of his palm like a roll of quarters.

One deep breath escaped Bayer's nostrils before he swung into action, anchoring a knee across the back of Holcomb's legs. The ex-detective barely had time to yell.

"What the fuck?!" Holcomb's words came out smothered as Bayer pushed his head deeper into the pillow underneath his head. A few quick punches to the ribs had Holcomb trying to curl into the fetal position to protect himself, but it was no use. The alcohol slowed his reflexes significantly compared to the beast pounding into him.

Blow after blow, Bayer laid into the cop who'd gotten his son kidnapped, beaten, and his daughter-in-law shot. There wouldn't be any mercy or forgiveness. Once Bayer grew hot with sweat beading down the side of his face, he knew it was time to go. He pulled Holcomb's unconscious and battered body off the bed, happy to see a bloodless sheet. He'd kept every blow concentrated to the torso. Bayer nodded a silent thank you to his gloved hands before walking the asshole out of the room and stood him up at the top of the stairs.

"A son for a son. You should have just left me

alone," Bayer mumbled to him before letting him go to fall down the steep flight of steps until he hit the front door with a thud.

Bayer placed the empty glass of Bourbon on the post of the banister at the top of the stairs and retraced his steps making sure to wipe down everywhere he stepped that night. He left the same way he came. He was done, and with his beast satiated, he walked away from Leon Holcomb's home with plans of never being in that man's personal space again.

The Slow Roast Diner sat on a random block somewhere in Long Island, about ten minutes away from the house Holcomb lived in. Bayer walked onto the back lot from a dark street and pulled out a set of keys that didn't belong to him to open a door of a car he didn't own. His heart rate slowly began to drop to normal levels as he fished out a laptop from a bag in the front passenger seat. He pulled his gloves off and checked his hands for any potential bruising. No scratches or any signs of struggle he could see.

After he powered on the computer, it only took a few keystrokes to wipe out the alarm key entry data showing the alarm never reactivated once Holcomb returned home. Bayer scrubbed his digital footprints just as thoroughly as the physical ones traipsing through the unconscious detective's home. When he was certain he'd completed his task, he headed through a backdoor into the diner.

The place was practically empty outside of a waitress, the cook, and the hostess. In fact, the three employees barely looked twice around the place as Bayer came out of a long hallway where the neon restroom sign buzzed above his head before sputtering out and blazing back on with a glowing red fury. He sat in a booth with an unfinished plate of chili cheese fries across the table from Penny "Pinch" Benziger. Bayer passed a set of car keys to the officer under the table.

"I told you not to eat those fries, man," the cook shouted at Bayer while shaking his head. "I got some Pepto in the back if you need it."

"Look at him, Carl," the waitress sighed and grabbed a pitcher of ice water, "He's all sweaty and shit. I told you to throw that damn chili out yesterday."

"It's not the chili, Diane," Carl, the cook, protested. "It's those damn day-old fries you keep refrying. Told ya we should be using fresh potatoes."

"And who's gonna peel fresh potatoes?" Diane screeched as if the task were beneath her.

Pinch simply snickered as he leaned back into the booth while the cook and the waitress continued to argue about food that shouldn't be fed to rats, let alone humans.

"All good?" Bayer asked his parole officer.

Pinch moved his head up and down slowly, "I don't want to know, but we've been here since about ten for a late meeting after you just finished a job for Rankin nearby. I imagine the car is in the same spot you found it in?"

"Yeah," Bayer said while looking down at the plate of cold food. He didn't dare touch it even though his appetite raged for something good to eat.

Pinch must have read his mind as he whispered to him, "Come on, let's get the hell out of here and grab some real food. I think I'm gonna need a tetanus shot after sitting in this booth."

The officer and his parolee laughed as they left some cash for their bill and walked out of the diner without another word of what Bayer achieved that night.

Peace had finally found Bayer, and so did sleep. It was one of the best nights of sleep he had in a very long time. When he woke up the following morning to start his day, the first thing Bayer did was turn on the news. There wasn't anything mentioned about the most infamous cop in the city, not a headline or a single crawl across the bottom of the screen. He didn't need to see or hear about his handiwork, but a part of him thought it would be nice.

Instead of dwelling on what the world didn't know, Bayer showered and got ready for his day. When he stepped outside of his apartment building, Officer Genevieve Parsons sat inside her car with her eyes glued to her cell phone instead of paying attention to her surroundings. She yelped and clutched her chest when Bayer tapped on her window.

"Jesus Christ, you scared the shit out of me, Bayer!" she huffed, trying to catch her frantic breaths after rolling down the window.

"Good morning, Gen," Bayer laughed. "What

brings you all the way out here?"

"I got a call asking about you. Where were you last night, Bayer?" she said with worry in her voice.

Bayer looked at her, giving his best expression of confusion, "I worked on a job for Ava until about 9:30, and then I had a late dinner with my PO at a diner until about 11. Maybe midnight? You have to check with him for the time stamp. Why? What's going on?"

"Holcomb," she sighed, pinching the bridge of her nose. "He said you attacked him last night. He's got a concussion, a few broken ribs, and he said you made him look like he'd drunkenly fell down the stairs in his house. They're trying to get a hold of you."

"If Holcomb is breathing, that should be a clear sign I had nothing to do with it."

"Bayer, please don't say that out loud to

anyone else," Genevieve pleaded.

He shrugged his shoulders, "It's not a secret this guy's been on my ass and doing some real yippee-ki-yay shit to rope me into some conspiracy he's been harboring from a night over seven years ago. He's lucky it wasn't me who attacked him; he wouldn't be able to talk if it was. They really need to update that system. They should have called Pinch, I mean, Mr. Benziger."

"So you two are getting along well then? No issues?" she asked him.

"We get along well enough. I have no complaints. I want to talk more about Holcomb's accusations, but I have a feeling I'm about to be busy for the rest of the day with this bullshit. I should probably give my PO and Martin a call to get ahead of this thing. I really wish this Holcomb guy would just leave me alone."

Genevieve agreed, "I do too. As a matter of

fact, I'm thinking about getting everybody he's harassed to draft up a formal complaint, and maybe we can use this to get you off parole early. It's a lot harder to harass a free citizen. You want to get breakfast?"

He wanted to, more than anything, but he was still a man on a mission. He wouldn't be satisfied until Holcomb was out of his life for good. "I'm sorry, Gen. I want to, but we shouldn't. Not now, and honestly, I can't tell you when."

"Well, answer me this." Her big brown eyes pulled him closer to the car, where he rested his arms atop the opened window. She grinned at their closeness. "How did you get the name Bayer?"

"Let my mother tell it; I was the cure to all of her headaches. Although I'm pretty sure I caused more than I cured." He chuckled at the random memory from conversations long ago.

The silence thickened the tension between them, and before it morphed into a missed opportunity, Bayer took a chance leaning in to kiss her gently. It was the kind of kiss that almost made him change his mind about going to grab breakfast, but he didn't. It felt like a goodbye, and he was certain she felt it too.

The way she touched the side of his face when he finally pulled away told him everything he needed to know. He was still an asshole for letting one of the greatest women he'd ever known drive away from him. He didn't want to keep lying to her, so walking away wasn't just the right thing to do; it was the best thing for them both.

23

Somewhere on a random block in the Lower East Side of Manhattan was an apartment that housed a disgraced police officer as he nursed wounds no one believed came from Bayer Thompson. Leon Holcomb stood in a bathroom a touch bigger than a closet. The white tiles ran from the floor up to the peeling stucco ceiling, ruined by the lives of tenants before him. Dried rust-colored stains decorated the corners, and the incessant dripping from the tub's faucet annoyed him to the point where it sounded like a bass drum beating against the side of his head.

The mirror held spots of splattered paint that he somehow knew wouldn't come off, and still, he stared at his reflection. His tired brown eyes watered at the image in front of him. The knot on the side of his head pulsed a steady flow of pain that rang just behind his forehead.

Fighting the urge to smash the mirror, Holcomb hobbled out of the bathroom and stared at the room around him. A single full-sized bed sat in the center with a TV on the dresser directly in front of it. The kitchen was barely bigger than the bathroom by the front door, and there was a closet in another corner. There wasn't anything spectacular about the place, but it would do until he went to trial.

A pang of guilt and grief rippled through Holcomb's chest as the images of his partner and the times they shared together flashed across his mind. The memories faded rather instantly, replaced with disturbing replays of Israel's eyes rolling to the back of his head while suffering seizures until he died. The guilt was followed by the searing pain of a deep breath that forced his broken ribs to move. Every inch of his body ached.

The cast wrapped around his entire left leg made it agonizing to walk. Breaking the bone in his thigh was no easy feat, but Bayer ensured the most damage was inflicted on him, and Holcomb regretted ever pushing the convict over the edge. He glared miserably at the crutches leaned against the wall and he continued to hobble his way over toward the bed where he sat down.

The burnt orange paint of the room shrunk the space but the empty wall separating the bed from the kitchen gave him plenty of room to work. It held dozens of pictures and documents from the Sinclair investigation that he'd taken out of the precinct before he'd been permanently relieved of his duties. Holcomb resolved to bring Bayer and Sinclair to justice despite his current circumstances. He even held a whisper of an idea that closing the case would get his charges dropped. So he worked it feverishly as if he and Israel still shared an office at the one nine.

A large diagram of the syndicate's organization held Sinclair at the top with a blank sheet of paper next to his photo and the name Johnie Irish under it. That's when it dawned on Holcomb that his saving grace would be to discover the identity of Sinclair's so-called silent partner. He held onto this last shred of being a cop with every fiber of his being. Day into night, night into day, he worked the photos and case files, trying to figure out the biggest mystery plaguing the task force he once worked with.

It happened on a warm night when Holcomb opened the window in his tiny apartment only to hear the sounds of two women arguing on the street below. One of their voices carried up to him as the stranger yelled at her target, "If I was a man, I'd fucking kill you!"

The phrase felt like a punch to the gut as Holcomb realized the entirety of his investigation hinged on an assumption about Johnie Irish that had never been proven. A surge of energy rushed through him as he began thumbing through files looking for anything to substantiate his hypothesis. It was the first time happiness found him in months, years even. While he didn't know exactly what he was looking for, he'd know when he found it. The frantic search brought him to the night from years ago when Bayer Thompson killed two men defending a woman no one could identify.

The hunch tickling Holcomb's brain had him tossing papers and photos aside in desperate search of a single image he kind of remembered seeing. It taunted him, teasing him about a night he couldn't let go because the love of his life died a few hours after Bayer Thompson ruined his life.

That's when he saw it—a cloudy image of someone sitting in the club next to a much younger-looking Cesar Sinclair. Holcomb pulled the photo and taped it over the blank sheet of paper with the name Johnie Irish underneath it.

The only thing left for him to do was prove it. However, a knock at the door disrupted his investigation of this new lead.

Holcomb pushed himself off the bed and used everything within his grasp to steady himself until he reached the door without actually using the crutches given to him at the hospital. He yelled through the door once he reached it. "Who is it?"

"Mr. Holcomb, it's Eugene Edelman, your attorney."

Holcomb opened the door for his lawyer and his lawyer's associate to enter. The man wasn't intimidating in the slightest, with his height barely topping 5'5' and his suit looking too big for his slender frame. He clomped into the apartment with a slight bob of his head in sync with his steps, followed by another gentleman who seemed to be in much better shape.

Holcomb watched the two men scan the

apartment and couldn't help but notice his lawyer's associate staring at the wall of photos and documents. He felt a sense of achievement knowing that someone else saw his handiwork.

"Mr. Holcomb, this is Brendan. He'll be in charge of your personal security until the trial is over," Edelman told him with a quick sweep of his light brown hair out of his face.

Holcomb eyed Brendan from head to toe. "That's it? Just Brendan?"

Brendan turned away from the wall with a smirk, "Just me, Mr. Holcomb. I can assure you I'm one of the best."

"Who's paying for this?" Holcomb asked his lawyer.

"The same party who posted your bond and paid for my services," Edelman said, matter-of-factly.

"The union is really covering this?" Holcomb asked, cocking his head to the side.

Edelman ignored his question, allowing the ex-cop to believe he earned one last benefit from the union he'd paid into as an officer of 15 years. Instead, the lawyer assured him, "We're taking your concerns about your safety very seriously. We've worked to get you moved into this apartment, right? All you have to do is sit tight until your trial date. Now, I'm going to leave Brendan here to discuss how you two will work together, and I'll see you tomorrow morning, bright and early, in my office. We need to discuss our media strategy."

"Okay," Holcomb agreed. There weren't any more words exchanged between him and his lawyer, but Brendan's presence spoke louder than the silence filling the room. The suit fit the bodyguard perfectly. Its quality seemed above and beyond Edelman's pay grade. His hair was buzzed short, and his chiseled jaw clean-shaven. Soft green eyes scanned every inch of Holcomb's investigation board like he was committing it to memory.

Once the attorney left, he decided to get some more information. "So, Brendan, you got a last name?"

Brendan tossed Holcomb a smile, "Brooks."

"Brendan Brooks, how long have you been doing this?"

"If I'm honest, I've been doing personal security for nearly three years now, and I was pretty good at it."

The statement struck Holcomb as odd, so he pressed on, "Oh yeah? Was?"

"Yeah, up until a few months ago, but I'm getting back in the swing of things." Brendan shifted his attention away from Holcomb and pointed to the wall in front of him, "You figure all of this out?"

Holcomb's ego allowed him to be distracted into changing the subject, hobbling over to his crowning achievement. He explained the investigation and even his hunch about Johnie Irish. Holcomb couldn't ignore the grin on Brendan's face as he stared at the picture he posted over the elusive criminal's name. "What's so funny?"

Brendan pointed at the picture, "You realize that's not a Johnie, and I'm damn sure she ain't Irish."

Holcomb shrugged, "It's just a hunch, really. I haven't had a chance to look into it."

"Well, enough about that. Let's get into how we should work together. I want to go over your daily schedule and things like that. First, you got anything to drink?" Brendan asked with a slight chuckle.

"Some water and beers in the fridge," Holcomb tipped his head toward the small kitchen, refusing to leave his post in front of his wall of evidence.

Brendan nodded, "Thanks, you want one?"

"Yeah, I'll take a beer. Do me a favor and grab those pills off the counter for me too."

Holcomb went back to his theories and wall of mayhem that led him to genuine discovery. His eyes locked onto the picture of a young woman from a night long ago. So much so he didn't notice the gloved hand passing him an ice-cold beer can already open. The first sip down his throat felt refreshing, while the next held the after taste of something bitter, something that didn't belong. He took his eyes off of the picture and looked at the can in his hand.

The world around him spun much like the morning Israel died. The can of beer slipped from

Holcomb's hand onto the floor. An overwhelming feeling swept over his body and forced him to fall back onto the bed. He could have sworn he heard his own heartbeat slowing down to a dangerous pace. Every breath became harder and harder to take.

Tears welled in Holcomb's eyes and spilled down the sides of his face. He went to yell, but nothing came out. Every blink of his eyes forced more tears down his cheeks.

"Who? Why?" Holcomb barely squeaked out.

Brendan stood just out of Holcomb's reach but still managed to lean over him, "You truly have a one-track mind, Detective. So focused on one thing, one person, that you fail to see everything else around you. You managed to figure out who Johnie is but still haven't the slightest clue of who I am or who Eugene works for."

"What?" Holcomb was fading fast. He could

barely stomach the fear, the anxiety, the gut-wrenching poison that kept his body paralyzed and splayed across the bed.

Brendan smirked and pulled the latex gloves further down onto his hands. "I was a great bodyguard once, but that changed the night some asshole came out of the shadows behind a restaurant and killed my client, my friend, and knocked me unconscious. You should have killed me too."

Holcomb desperately wanted this to be a dream, a nightmare, something he could wake up from, but Holcomb would never wake up again.

*****

Silver Johnson-Sinclair sat next to her husband on a yacht floating off the coast of Miami, eating dinner served to them by their waitstaff while watching the evening news report. Holcomb's face flashed across the screen, which caused her to elbow Cesar, who was busy swiping through his phone.

"Breaking News, disgraced detective Leon Holcomb, was found in an apartment in the Lower East Side of Manhattan early this afternoon. Initial reports indicate suicide. He is survived by his parents, who our sources say is foregoing an autopsy, wanting to put their son to rest along with his past-"

Silver shut the TV off and returned to the plate of food in front of her while Cesar watched her for a moment.

"Was that you?" He asked her nonchalantly.

She shook her head slowly from side to side, cutting a bite-sized piece of rare steak and letting the reddish juices seep onto the plate. One small bite, and she closed her eyes to chew it slowly, enjoying the morsel like she'd never be able to eat steak again.

"It wasn't me, but I know who," she finally replied. However, her phone rang before she could say anything else.

Answering the call, the familiar voice of Biro Barnabas came through the other end of the line, "I need to speak to Irish."

Silver rolled her eyes and handed Cesar the phone, who put it on speaker and sat it on the table. "Go."

"Everything is cleaned up as promised. So we're done, yes?"

"We're done." Cesar disconnected the call and shot a look at his wife, who pushed her plate of food away. He could feel the heat from the anger bubbling up inside of her. "Why does he bother you so much?"

"You mean outside of the fact that he has direct contact with me? A man guided by his emotions is bad for business, mine especially."

"It was his son."

"That's the same reason you gave me about keeping Thompson alive," Silver sneered. "Killing them all would have solved all of my problems. Only dead men keep secrets."

Cesar took his wife's hand into his and kissed the top as if it would soothe the raging monster inside of her. "Thompson saved your life once upon a time. We need people like him to do the right thing. Not to mention, unleashing Johnie Irish would stir up an entirely new set of issues."

"Oh, for fuck's sake, not you too! Y'all need to let this Irish shit go," she side-eyed him before shaking her head and pulling her hand away. "You kill one guy with a bottle of Jameson, and they never let you forget it."

Thank You

For

Reading

Please leave a review &

Go to phoenixjonespublishing.com for new

releases and our entire catalog.

Made in the USA
Monee, IL
19 July 2021

73900841R00148